# Anson's Way

# Anson's Way

## By Gary D. Schmidt

sandpiper

HOUGHTON MIFFLIN HARCOURT
BOSTON NEW YORK

All rights reserved. Published in the United States by Sandpiper, an imprint
of Houghton Mifflin Harcourt Publishing Company. Originally published in
hardcover in the United States by Clarion, an imprint of Houghton Mifflin
Harcourt Publishing Company, 1999.

SANDPIPER and the SANDPIPER logo are trademarks of Houghton Mifflin
Harcourt Publishing Company.

For information about permission to reproduce selections from this book,
write to Permissions, Houghton Mifflin Harcourt Publishing Company, 215
Park Avenue South, New York, New York 10003.

www.sandpiperbooks.com

The text of this book is set in 12-point Adobe Caslon.

The Library of Congress has cataloged the hardcover edition as follows:
Schmidt, Gary D.
Anson's way / by Gary D. Schmidt.
p. cm.
Summary: While serving as a British Fencible to maintain the peace
in Ireland, Anson finds that his sympathy for a hedge master places him
in conflict with the law of King George II.
1. Ireland—History—18th century—Juvenile fiction. [1. Ireland—History—
18th century—Fiction. 2. Fathers and sons—Fiction. 3. Identity—Fiction.]
I. Title.
PZ7.S3527Ke    1999
[Fic]—dc21   98-29220
CIP
AC

ISBN 978-0-395-91529-5
ISBN 978-0-547-23761-9 pa

Manufactured in the United States of America
QUM 10 9 8 7 6 5 4 3 2 1

*for Steve and Viola Van Der Weele,*
*who plant straight hedgerows*

# Anson's Way

# The Hedge Master

In a small sod house scooped out beneath an embankment of hedges, a master teaches fifteen or sixteen students. Sometimes there are more, sometimes fewer, depending upon the farm season. The house—if it might be called a house—is invisible against the embankment. Nevertheless, one boy stands hidden on guard.

Inside, the children sit on rounded stones. Each has brought two sods for the peat fire, and they are stacked in a pile by the corner. Moving from group to group, the hedge master listens to recitations, nodding and correcting. The children share the Latin and Greek books. Afterward, before his students leave separately to avoid being seen, he tells them a tale out of Ireland's past. A tale, perhaps, of High King Brian Boru, or of the sorties of Goffraidh O'Donnell, or of Cuchulain and his spear of dragon bone. He speaks in the music of their own tongue.

He is violating something close to a score of King George II's laws.

In England, he is said to be teaching superstition and the evil customs of his nation—the seeds of Irish rebellion.

To keep those seeds from rooting, England has hoed away Irish laws, Irish ways, Irish names, the Irish language itself. No one may tell an Irish tale. There are to be no schools, no places of learning, no teachers, no lawyers.

There are to be no Catholic churches, no priests, no saying of the Mass, even if it means hell itself for the papists. It is believed that the Irish kneel down in their homes at the hour Mass is being said in Rome, but no Englishman has seen this.

Yet it is not enough to attack only the soul of a people. England does more. No Irishman may own a horse of value. No Irishman may apprentice to a gunsmith. No Irishman may travel abroad for schooling.

And no Irishman may own the fields he works. Families that have lived for generation upon generation on the same land find their acreage suddenly claimed by a gentleman in London who has never seen it. They are tenants in their own houses and might be removed at any moment. Half, perhaps more, of the oats, potatoes, cabbages, and wheat they grow goes to their rent and is shipped to England to make the London gentleman wealthier.

It is in these times that the hedge masters teach, under threat of imprisonment, fine, exile to Australia, and execution. Behind hedgerows, in barns, in caves, in hovels with little or no roof, they set up their schools. And the children come. Secretly and quietly, the children come to learn of their own forbidden world.

# 1

Anson Granville Staplyton, the seventh Staplyton to take up the noblest pursuit of defending the realm, toppled onto the deck of His Majesty's ship *Fortune*. He held his pale hand to a face that was usually blushing. Today it was green. Wildly he looked about, then bolted to the side of the ship and sputtered his breakfast into the Irish Sea. He had chosen the wrong side, and what remained of the meaty pudding, breast of duck, currant scones, and heady ale he had finished off that morning spattered across the newly painted black hull.

"Blast you for a lubber, boy! With the wind, not into it. With the wind." This from the second mate, who had brought enough young gentlemen across on His Majesty's ships to no longer care whether they lived or died as long as they did not mar his paint. "A limber-kneed lubber!" he hollered again and, shaking his head, went to find a ship's boy he could let down over the side to clean so the *Fortune* would not be shamed when she dropped anchor in Dublin Bay.

Anson held two lines, taut as sabers, that soared off to the masts above him. Their straining against the wind sent a thrill down into his arms, but he hardly noticed. When the ship's head ducked down to the sea, he let go and staggered across decks, bending his knees against the roll and rushing at the last before the deck bucked up into the next wave. With the wind this time. He marveled that there could be anything left in his stomach. He hoped he would die soon.

A touch on his shoulder, and he turned to the pocked face of Sergeant Eyre. "Forty-odd year I've been in such crossing, forty-odd year, and I still remember my first time like it was yesterday morning. Keep your eye out to the west. No, the west. What looks blue and isn't moving are the hills below Dublin. Keep those in your eye, and your stomach will stand to rights."

Anson gulped and nodded. "I didn't expect to cross in a storm."

"A storm, you say? A storm? By all love, after this day, you'll never see its like. The ship hardly needs a helm, as calm as it is." Sergeant Eyre clapped him on the shoulder and strolled forward, chuckling, his feet as sure as if they were walking across Gadshall Green. "A storm, he says!"

Anson wiped his mouth with the back of his hand. The

wind cooled the sweat on his neck and chilled him, but he clung to the ship's side and kept his eyes on the steady blue at the horizon's edge. Above him the wind shrilled against the rigging while the big-bellied sails shoved the ship up and across perfect mountains of gray-green water. Could the ship not run with the waves for a time? Anson wondered. But it did not. The blue hills below Dublin seemed no nearer.

If he had been less intent on keeping the horizon in his sight, he might have heard the steel-toed approach behind him.

"Mr. Staplyton!" Anson wheeled around and almost fell. Quickly he ran a hand through his hair. If only the salty air had flattened the tight curls that plagued him . . .

"Mr. Staplyton." The growl of Colonel Staplyton was low and huge. "You are unable to recall your orders?"

He did recall them. "I am to remain below, sir."

"You are to remain below. And are you inclined to follow those orders?"

"I am, sir."

"Very good, Mr. Staplyton." He turned forward. "Sergeant Eyre. Sergeant!"

The sergeant marched to them as though he were on parade. He did not look at Anson. "Sir."

"Sergeant, you will see to it that this man goes below. You will see to it that he stays below." A slight, ever so slight nod of his head to Anson, then with godlike ease, the colonel turned his back and walked away, his hands clasped behind him.

Sergeant Eyre took Anson under the arms and helped him struggle to the hold. They waited for the right pitch to clamber below, and when it came, the sergeant half lifted him down the stairway. The dark, lit only by the glimmer of oil lamps, was as noxious as when he had left, and Anson felt another retch in his throat. Down the last three steps, and Sergeant Eyre released him at the bottom. "Eat this, Drummer," he said, holding out an apple. "It's a bit punky, I'll grant you, but there's nothing like it against the seasickness."

Anson took it and, keeping his head low against the deck beams, lurched from post to post to find his kit. He closed his eyes and tried again to imagine the blue hills, but the smothering air of the hold, the stench of human sweat and burned oil overpowered him. He settled down with his back to the hull, his head between his legs and his nails squeezed into his palms. The thought of the apple in his stomach appalled him.

I've waited for this day all my life, he thought, and here I am in it. Drummer with the Staffordshire Fencibles, just like my father, and his father, and his father before him. He wondered why they had never told him about the crossing. When the sea took a wicked pitch and slapped him back against the hull, he viciously hoped that they had all been as sick as he.

A week ago—just a very short week ago—he had walked in Staplyton Manor at Gadshall. His mother and three sisters had been weepy all day with the thought of him leaving. But dressed in the fine uniform of the Fencibles, he had pranced about the manor, practicing drum rolls and scattering the sheep. The glossy leather of the belts across his chest, the bright red and white of his coat and breeches, the burnished copper of the buckles, the black sheen of the spatterdashes buttoned up and down his legs— he had strutted them all.

"Anson," his mother had said, her hand to her cheek, "you might have been a rector. Think of your grandfather Berkeley and the serenity of his parish."

"Mother," answered Anson severely, "all that Grandfather does is read."

"There is pleasure in reading too, Anson."

"No Staplyton has ever been a rector," said Anson. He was sure that this was true. He had heard his father say it often enough.

On the morning he was to go, he begrudged the delay in saying farewell. Eager to reach Liverpool and his father, the colonel, and to begin his grand career, he endured his mother's stifling, teary hug, shook his sisters' hands, and stepped into the Staplyton coach, remembering only at the last moment to reach outside for a final wave.

He had found his father his usual self: a quick, scathing look up and down, an adjustment of his son's coat, a pointing out that the Staffordshire Fencibles did not generally carry the dust of their county on their boots. When the colonel finally approved, Anson had marched to stand with the veteran Fencibles, holding himself as straight as if he had a ruler down his back, always aware of his father's terrible eye upon him. Then came the sign for his drum roll— a finger in the air—and he had tripled it perfectly, holding the cadence with an admirable steadiness until the fifes had shrilled in and the muster was dismissed to its barracks.

Anson had looked to catch his father's eye, but the colonel had already turned to his own quarters and showed his son nothing but his broad back.

Six more days of drilling and waiting, until Anson felt the vibration of the drum in his head and his palms had molded themselves around the sticks. Six days of being up before sunrise and summoning the muster, of vying for kidney beans and wheat bread—the good, hard stuff on which a Fencible marches. Six days of polishing and repolishing, of envying the other Fencibles their muskets, of breathing in the white powder of the officers' wigs.

And six days of a terrible and unexpected loneliness. Whenever his grandfather Staplyton had spoken of the Fencibles—and there was precious little else he did speak of—he spoke about camaraderie, the closeness that came between men under fire, the loyalty of one Fencible to another. But in those first few days, Anson was more alone than he had ever been. He was the son of the colonel, and so the other Fencibles held him at a distance, waiting to see not only how he would be preferred but if they would prefer him themselves.

At night, Anson lay in the dark, regretting his last moments at Staplyton Manor and wishing that he could be playing summer games with his sisters, even though he was a Staffordshire Fencible.

But now in the bowels of the *Fortune*, he held his head low in his hands and hoped that no one would see a Fencible shudder.

"On deck. On deck. Fencibles on deck. Drummer, to the muster! To the muster!"

Anson swiped his face, slung his kit across his back, and rounding the drum with both arms, skittered across the hold, stepping to avoid the curses that came his way when the *Fortune* flung him against another Fencible. He fought a slant of the stairs and fell out on his knees upon the deck, the tar of the deck seams smearing a line across his best black spatterdashes.

"Drummer, to the muster!" called out Sergeant Eyre, and Anson hobbled across the deck to his place just below the poop, hoping the tar would not show against the leggings. If it did, the colonel gave no sign. Anson set his feet wide and flared the drum roll. It sounded unnaturally weak in the sea air but was strengthened by the thudding of Fencibles gushing from the hold, white and red and perfect in their uniforms, dashing to their places and toeing a deck seam to stand as straight as straight could be. With the last Fencible, the colonel lifted a finger to stop the drum, and Anson dropped his arms to his sides, index fingers pointing rigidly down to his ankles. A whistle trilled the air, and the *Fortune* entered Dublin Bay.

Anson had expected this to be a grand moment: pennants flying, brass trim glistening, new sails flour white and taut. Here was the might of England, the pride of the world. Out of the sea breezes and in water stilled by low cliffs and strands, the *Fortune* coasted into the bay, the Fencibles growing more rigid as the lines on the sails loosened.

Anson kept his eyes past the masts and to the spires that thrust themselves up into the sky. He could not help but follow the antic flying of the gulls—hundreds and hundreds of gulls—that shrieked and cackled them into the River Liffey, where they would dock. The *Fortune* wallowed from side to side as the seawall bounced waves back to it, but Anson kept his footing—just like the rigid colonel. A splash at the bow—"Give way, there. There, give way!"—and the *Fortune* settled herself into the water with a jerk, letting her own wake catch and pass her and flow on and on into the heart of Dublin.

The sailors flurried all around them, securing the ship to the limestone seawall along the North Quay, while the Fencibles stood, red-coated statues, waiting for the order to disembark. The colonel, hands still clasped behind his back, prowled the ship's poop, and Anson watched for the movement of the finger that would signal his next drum roll.

"Give way, there. Way, way, lubber, or you'll draw her into the quay! Boom here and fend her off. Off!" Anson was grateful that the second mate's orders were not directed at him.

He pushed up on his toes to look at the port, the entry to which had claimed his breakfast. If it had been hell's gates themselves that he saw, Anson would hardly have quailed, so glad was he to have the deck quiet under his feet. Still, he had hoped for more than this. It looked to be a place where rats could make free, and the scurrying he had seen in just a single glance suggested that they did. The gray, dingy stone walls of the quay—the high-water mark on them a line of scum and weed and filth—led further into a gray, dingy city. The buildings beyond rose shadowed and shuttered, and the one or two open windows on top stories looked like wounded, sightless eyes, unlit and secret. Anson was not sure that he wanted to know what went on in those rooms. Below them hunched an emporium of shops; cordage, ship's stores, spars, sails, dunnage belched out their doorways. Though the sun was high, the street along the quay was dark and cold, deserted but for a gang of sailors. Anson shivered in the shadows cast across the river.

"Mr. Staplyton!"

The colonel's eyes glared at him, and quickly Anson's drumsticks began to roll. Two sailors shored open the ship's side and shoved the gangway down to the quay; then they all stood back to allow the officers to descend to the streets of Ireland. Colonel Staplyton passed Anson coldly. "Your leggings are disgraceful. Fall in behind." Two by two the Fencibles followed, a solid and formidable phalanx as strong, thought Anson, as the king's own hand, giving order to his people. If only he would prove to be as formidable and strong himself.

Their feet moving in time with Anson's snaring, the Fencibles marched in a slow and orderly line along the quay. They crossed a bridge that leaped across the River Liffey in five elegant arches, and then hunched together down through the dark, winding, narrow streets of Dublin, so narrow that two Fencibles walking side by side might reach out to the opposing houses whose fronts stared so darkly at them. Anson wondered if this was all that Dublin would offer.

But then a sudden opening brought Anson into the light and air of a market street, and dingy warehouses gave way to the columned porticoes and filigreed spires of the university. Everywhere there were shops spilling wares out onto the street; bells and chants of hawkers; actors tumbling in front of small crowds, their costumed dogs barking at the antics; ladies holding their skirts above the churned mud. Fruit sellers called out the excellence of last autumn's withered apples, of their gooseberries and blackthorn sticks. Bookstores, flower stalls, clothiers, poultry shops with unplucked chickens dangling by their claws in the windows, apothecaries, barbers, tearooms, and fishmongers all rollicked together in a great hubbub that stilled for a moment as the Fencibles marched past and then closed in again behind them as though they had never been there at all.

Other than Liverpool, it was the largest city Anson had ever seen. It could hardly have been more distinct from the sleepy stucco of Gadshall. The shops, he supposed, were as alike as any that might be found in England. But there was a brooding about the place that told him England was well behind him. He would pass by a green where English sheep mulched and English soldiers trained, and then, just beyond, he would see a convent doorway with a statue of the Blessed Virgin serenely watching, or a monastery chapel with its gory painting of a crucifix, the blood of the dying Christ spouting in a bright red. Everywhere, he saw houses whose gables sharpened into small stone crosses, or limestone walls marked by brass plaques with sacred symbols. The God of his Puritan chapel at home was suddenly a foreigner, and Anson was glad that he had the familiar thrumming of the drums to keep him in the right world.

Past Trinity Chapel, its bronze bells still so new as not to have entirely greened, and on to New Barracks at last. Here everything was familiar. The red coats of the Staffordshire Fencibles blended with the red coats of Fifeshire Fencibles, Yorkshire Foot Guards, and Herefordshire Light Dragoons. The colonel mustered the Fencibles on the quadrangle before the barracks, eyeing them for the slightest misstep and pushing up an eyebrow when he saw one. A raised finger, and Anson stilled the drum.

"Staffordshire Fencibles," came the low growl of the colonel's voice, "you have come to Ireland to keep the king's peace. God knows what would happen if the swinish multitude that inhabits this corner of His Majesty's dominion should ever take up arms against civilization. It is accorded the duty of the Fencibles here gathered that no one else should ever know." A pause, perhaps to allow for laughter.

"There are those who not only endeavor to withdraw His Majesty's subjects from their obedience but wish to alter their very natures, to stir up sedition and rebellion to the great hazard of the ruin and desolation of this kingdom. It is our role to defend His Majesty's realm.

"I know that every man here will do his duty. I know that every man here will keep the peace. I know that every man here will be loyal to God and king. And as God is my life, I know that every man here will be loyal to the death to every other Staffordshire Fencible. God save His Royal Grace."

And at this, Anson found himself cheering until the new bells of Trinity Chapel rang.

"Fencibles dismissed," called the colonel, and then turned to his own quarters.

Confusion ruled the rest of the day. As the drummer, Anson was the last to be assigned a place. It was almost nightfall before Sergeant Eyre found him a bunk—one in an unfortunate corner whose stained ceiling and missing stucco suggested that a rainy night would mean a wetting. He threw his kit beneath the bunk, his drum on top, and raced to salvage the last of the mess—beef and dried peas. Then, suddenly tired beyond tired, he returned to fall instantly and dreamlessly asleep on the horsehair mattress. No matter that it smelled as if the hair had not long ago been separated from its owner.

Anson soon found that whether in Liverpool or Dublin, the colonel would drill his men again and again. One day it was wheeling and facing, with the entire regiment marching stiff kneed at seventy-five steps to the minute. At the colonel's silent signal, Anson increased the beat to one hundred twenty steps a minute, with the regiment wheeling and facing, wheeling and facing until they seemed in a perfect whirl.

Another day it was musket drill, the only drill that did not proceed to Anson's drumming. He too was assigned a musket and fumbled at Sergeant Eyre's barking.

"Hand to cartridge!" Sergeant Eyre shouted, and each Fencible drew a cartridge from the belt at his waist.

"Prime and charge! No, Staplyton, first the powder, then the paper, then the cartridge. Powder, paper, cartridge.

"Draw rammer and ram cartridge! Poise firelock! Cock firelock! Take aim! Fire!"

Even the explosion that followed did not cover the din of Sergeant Eyre's voice. "I suppose this regiment will do well if it has to fire at something larger than all of London. But God save us if we are to fire against another regiment. Now. Poise firelock! Handle cartridge!" And so on and on through the long daylight hours until every single Fencible was glad to see Anson pick up his sticks and beat the tattoo, ordering everyone into quarters.

Colonel Staplyton never spoke to Anson in any way other than as colonel to drummer, and truth to tell, Anson was glad. Those watching to see if he would be preferred relented, and he felt himself being drawn into the Fencibles. He was no longer "the new drummer," or even "the colonel's son," but "young Staplyton." Young Staplyton began to find a place saved for him at the mess. The stock of beef that would have been taken first was now left on the trencher for him. And on a night when Ireland opened up her gray skies and let loose a deluge that would have impressed Noah himself, Corporal Oakes switched bunks with Anson and spent the night dodging the soggy stucco that fell in chunks.

In the hours that did not include mustering, drilling, polishing, or readying his kit for inspection by one of the lieutenants, Anson accompanied the patrols that footed themselves sternly around the streets of Dublin. He had never imagined a city like this. The sheer cackle and noise of the place was heady. Despite his resolve that his face should be as stolid as that of his father, he caught himself more than once gaping at the street fairs, the park theaters, the sea captains with strange-skinned pineapples for sale, or the pubs whose brewery breath seasoned the air.

"Close your mouth, young Staplyton," warned Lieutenant Fielding. "The colonel would more than box your ears if you was to be caught in such a place."

"But I had not thought of going in, sir."

"See that the thought does not come upon you, then."

Sometimes they patrolled as far as Phoenix Park, and if it was Lieutenant Fielding in command, he would wave his drummer off for an hour. Anson would dash into the light woods, scattering the deer that did not seem to know that they were grazing in the center of a city. There would be an hour of clouds and grass and thickened trees with beckoning branches, and he would be Anson of Gadshall again and not a Staffordshire Fencible at all. At the bell tones that Trinity Chapel spread over all of Dublin, he would straighten his uniform and sprint back to the patrol waiting at the Conyngham Road gate.

"A good hour, young Staplyton?"

"Thank you, sir. A good hour indeed."

But if Lieutenant Brockle was commanding, there would be no good hour. As they patrolled past the park, Anson would try not to let his longing eyes stray from the straight and narrow back of the lieutenant, though smelling the expanse of lawn and lake that called to him so sweetly of home.

It was Lieutenant Brockle one morning who ripped

away his blanket and startled him to a day that had yet to be born. "Drummer. Drummer. Wake up, boy. Muster on the quadrangle in a quarter hour. A quarter hour, do you hear?"

"A quarter hour, sir."

Lieutenant Brockle strode off. Anson wondered why he had his sword strapped to his side so early in the morning.

Anson dropped his feet to the cold stone floor, lifted them once, sighing, and then stepped over to Corporal Oakes. "Sir, there's to be a muster, sir. In just a quarter hour. Shall I wake the regiment, sir?"

"A devil of a morning to wake a regiment this early. God's death, Mr. Staplyton, cannot it wait until the sun has decided to rise?"

"Lieutenant Brockle himself, sir, came to wake me."

"Lord, if Lieutenant Brockle himself came to wake you, we'd best pipe to."

And pipe to they did. Even before Anson was standing ramrod straight in the rain, beating out a morning muster, most of the Fencibles had staggered past their last morning dreams and presented themselves sharply, more or less. One of the straps behind Corporal Oakes's back was twisted, and two of the Fencibles' spatterdashes not buttoned up fully at the knees, but the rain was steady enough for Anson to doubt there would be a full inspection.

Lieutenants Fielding and Brockle stood side by side across the quadrangle, the white powder of their wigs washing down to the red of their coats. But they stood so still and so sternly that no one would have thought of noticing. When the colonel strode from his quarters and across the quadrangle, they drew their sabers and fell in behind him. Anson saw that the rain had instantly splashed mud onto the colonel's leggings. He had never seen them so before.

At the far end of the quadrangle, hard by the wall that surrounded New Barracks, a wooden pillar rose out of the cobblestones, dark and slick in the rain. The colonel motioned for a slow roll, and as Anson's hands lowered and began, four men marched slowly from the guardhouse. Two wore the red of the Fencibles, one wore a most respectable dark-gray coat, but the fourth wore only a shirt and brown breeches. The rain will soak him through, thought Anson.

Water poured off the brims of the Fencibles' hats as Anson's roll continued. The four marched slowly across the quadrangle in procession, until they reached the pillar, stopped, and turned to face the muster.

The colonel's voice menaced the gray air. "To teach the Irish tongue is treason against our king. To teach papist cant for the purpose of inciting rebellion is treason against our king. The punishment for such treason is death."

Anson found himself suddenly shaking.

"But the king, God save him, is merciful. He will not suffer treason, but neither will he suffer his people to feel the brunt of anger. The sentence for Owen Roe Sullivan is commuted to thirty lashes." The colonel folded his hands behind his back. "Drummer, by the condemned."

Struggling to control his shivering, Anson marched carefully to the pillar, his legs numbed.

"Proceed, Lieutenant Fielding."

A long hesitation. "Sir, thirty lashes in a rain like this . . ."

"I must agree," said the man in the gray coat. "In all my years in His Majesty's navy, no man was ever lashed in such a rain."

"This is not His Majesty's navy, Dr. Hoccleve, and the liberties enjoyed by a surgeon and his commanding officer on board ship are not to be entertained among the Staffordshire Fencibles." The colonel wheeled his head about. "Proceed, Lieutenant Fielding."

Stiffly, the lieutenant strode to the pillar. He took the rope held out by one of the Fencibles and looped it around the condemned man's hands and then, turning him, knotted it around the pillar. He reached to the back of the man's shirt and with a tear ripped it open. Then he stepped back as the other Fencible drew off his coat and took a dangling whip from his belt.

"Drummer," shouted the colonel through the rain. "Roll."

And as Anson began a low, steady roll, the Fencible took his stance, swung the whip twice over his shoulder, and then flashed it through the air to snap loudly on the condemned man's back. The man jerked, then arched himself to receive the next. The Fencible drew the tails of the whip between the fingers of his left hand and shook the flesh and blood to the cobblestones.

"One," said Lieutenant Fielding.

A second flash, a second jerk, and Anson's hands faltered, his fingers cold and white. "Drummer," came the warning voice of the colonel, and Anson felt the gorge rising in him.

"Two," said Lieutenant Fielding.

Anson looked at the back of the man, at the two red gashes that cut through the skin and laid bare the stippled muscle beneath. Then the whip flashed again and the muscle disappeared in a spurt of blood, a terrible spurt of blood that the rain quickly washed down in a stained sheet.

"Three," said Lieutenant Fielding.

Under the inexorable eye of the colonel, the whip flashed again and again, again and again, and Lieutenant Fielding's count went on and on, and the drum roll hefted into the air until Anson felt as if he had never been doing anything else, that Gadshall was a dream, that he had always been standing by the terrible pillar. A surge of hot hatred filled him. He hated the man whose back was being torn behind him. He hated the blood that even now stained the cobblestones at his feet. He hated him for the rain, for the cold, for the shivering that he could not stop. And Anson hated him for not screaming out at the lash, for suffering with only a low moan, for bearing what no man should bear.

"Thirty," said Lieutenant Fielding, and Anson's hands froze to a stillness.

The Fencible standing by cut the rope. The man fell to his knees, then full forward onto the stones. When Anson looked, he could see nothing but the tatters of skin where his back had been, the rain washing at it.

His hands still behind his back, the colonel strode forward. "It is at my word that the king's mercy came. My word. This you will remember."

Slowly, slowly, impossibly, the man pushed himself up against the pounding of the rain. Anson stared, as though something supernatural were happening on this very quadrangle, before his very eyes. Slowly, slowly the man raised his head and spoke raspingly, the words hardly able to get through the throat. "Ireland . . ." He coughed, almost fell, and caught himself. "Ireland will be remembering the king's mercy."

The colonel stared at him for a moment, then turned away.

"Lieutenant Fielding, take care of this man. Lieutenant Brockle, dismiss the men to breakfast. We'll have no more of hedge masters this day."

Later, Anson remembered that this was the first moment he had heard of a hedge master.

CHAPTER

2

$\mathcal{F}$or a week the skies of Ireland poured rain down upon the Fencibles, cold, sheeting rain that would not be stopped. When they drilled on St. Stephen's Green, it soaked their uniforms and kept them shivering between marches. When they mustered on the quadrangle, it dulled the drum rolls. The Fencibles came to attention in ankle-deep puddles, the rain spattering off the slate roof of New Barracks, clattering down the gutters, and pouring in a gritty stream out onto the quadrangle. It scoured the stones and washed away all the blood.

When Corporal Oakes grew surly and ordered Anson back to his own soggy bunk, there was hardly a thing Anson owned that was not wet.

During one of these days of rain, Anson was summoned to Colonel Staplyton's quarters. Though he was able to find reasonably dry and clean clothing, the short run across the puddles of the quadrangle spotted his leggings. Hell and damnation, he thought as he knocked. He hoped he could keep them out of the colonel's line of sight.

He could not. The colonel saw them instantly. "Drummer . . ." he began, exasperated.

"Sir, they were clean not two moments ago. If you will permit me—"

The colonel waved his hand. "I fear that I must acclimate myself to an eternity of besotted leggings. But to other matters. Boy, you will understand that I am unable to entertain you in these quarters. I will not be charged with favoritism."

"I understand, sir."

The colonel nodded. "There is this from your mother. I supposed you would care to see it." He handed Anson a letter. The rounded letters of his name scripted so carefully on the envelope called to him of home as surely as if he were stepping across the threshold itself. He could see his mother leaning over her writing desk, the lamplight on her gentle, thin hands. He could see her delicate dipping of the pen into the ink, then her tapping of it against the bottle so that she would not blot. He could even see her blowing gently against the paper before she folded it.

"No need to fear," said the colonel. "All well at home. Yes, I have a letter too. She asks about you. She asks whether you have become a Fencible. How shall I answer?"

"Tell her, sir, that I am indeed a Fencible."

A small smile from the colonel. "It is no easy thing,

especially for the colonel's son. And you did well at the flogging."

"Thank you, sir."

"If you had fallen in a heap, you would not have been the first Fencible to do so."

Anson paused. He wanted to savor the pleasure of his father's praise. "The lashing was terrible, sir."

"It was. It must be. Let him spread his papist ways outside Dublin, and before the year is out, there will be a Catholic army raised in Ireland to match the Catholic army in France, and England squeezed tight between them."

"The hedge master was brave during the lashing, sir."

The colonel picked up another letter from his desk. "He was," he said quietly, then slid a small knife through the wax seal and opened it. "Dismissed, Drummer. Tend to the leggings."

Anson left the colonel's quarters. The rain was spattering down as hard as it ever had. It did him no good to try to clear the puddles; the quadrangle was a single sheet of Irish rain. But Anson hardly cared. He had an hour, perhaps a bit more, before the next muster. And there was his mother's letter to read.

He read it often in the next week. Between wet inspections and wetter musters, between practicing his drumbeats and scrubbing his leggings, he read it again and again. It brought his mother's voice to New Barracks, and he heard her telling of the petit sins of his sisters, of the early yellow in the garden, of visiting aunts and uncles, of the minor skirmishes of the parish. He wondered why he had never noticed how sweetly scented all these were.

When he woke on the eighth day, Anson was sure that the sun must have drowned. The hairy blanket of the sky was bulging with the whole of the Irish Sea, splitting at its seams with the weight. It was more than Corporal Oakes could bear. "Damn and blast," he swore. "Moss will be sprouting on us next, if we've not grown fins and gills first." He twisted the tails of his coat and let out a stream of stained water. "Why in God's name we should be in Ireland at all is more than I can answer."

He had not seen Lieutenant Brockle at the door behind him.

"Corporal," came the lieutenant's voice, slow and menacing.

Corporal Oakes whirled about.

"Is it your opinion that the king's duty is to be undertaken only where it suits you?"

"No indeed, sir."

"And is it your opinion that the king's duty is to be undertaken only when you are warm and tipping a tankard by a fire?"

"No, sir."

"Just right, Corporal. Just right. The reason in God's name that we should be here is that the Irish are a savage race, incapable of recognizing a kindness, resistant to all lawful rule, fanatical in their religion, and willing to be led into every disorder by their priests. We are here to govern those who are incapable of governing themselves, an intemperate people who are without foresight or prudence, who are as changeable as birds and act only by impulse."

"I understand, sir. My apologies."

"So, Corporal Oakes, if it is the king's will that you should be in Ireland?"

"Then I accept that will wholeheartedly, sir."

Lieutenant Brockle nodded. "He will be pleased to hear it. Presently it is the king's will, Corporal, that you take a squad—your choice—and stand hard by the entrance to St. Stephen's Green until I send for you again."

"Yes, sir. St. Stephen's Green."

"Choose your men and be gone within the quarter hour."

It was to Corporal Oakes's credit that not a single man in the regiment shrank from volunteering. And Anson was proud to stand through the long morning, through the longer afternoon, and well into the darkness with the other seven Fencibles whom the corporal chose. They came back to a place of honor around the coal stove and mugs of piping hot cider. And Anson found that the leak over his bed had been repaired.

One morning, just when it seemed as if Dublin itself must sink, the clouds pulled back and left a sky as perfectly blue and round as any that could be imagined. When Anson came out of New Barracks, the wet still dripped from the eaves, but every drop prismed in the sunlight, and the breeze that blew out of the opened sky was green in its freshness. Corporal Oakes, who was careful to say nothing more of the weather, grinned like a schoolboy when he rousted the Fencibles out to the muster.

Even the colonel seemed pleased—and there was cause.

"Fencibles, you will repair to the barracks by rank and prepare for a march. Full gear. Officers, you will see to dry powder. It is time that the king got the value of the good rations he sends to the Fencibles every day. Muster in the half hour."

Quickly the regiment broke into ranks. They dragged packs from beneath the bunks and filled them with shot and new powder brought from the gunnery. They brought hardtack from the kitchens. They hastily cleaned rifle bores again and slid bayonets beneath. Belting their sabers and looping their pack belts over their shoulders, the Fencibles heard one word rushing through the barracks: "Outlaw."

Anson tensed when he heard it. After all the drills, to be finally marching against an enemy of the king tightened his stomach with excitement.

Anson drummed the regiment into a double line, and to his beat the Fencibles marched down the Conyngham Road and past Phoenix Park, startling the deer to a run with their proud stepping. After the last house along the road, they marched between long hedgerows planted atop stone-and-sod banks that divided the fields. The hedges had grown so high and thick over years and years that they were impenetrable, and the sheen of the Fencibles' red coats heated the trapped air between them. Had Anson paused in his drumming and looked back, he would have seen steam rising wispily from soggy cocked hats and woolen uniforms.

The sun rose and the country grew barer. Cabbage rows and fields of winter wheat yielded to bogs, stretching out flat except for the strange and almost frightening rocks that thrust themselves out of the green mire like men strangling for breath. Anson shuddered at the thought of sinking beneath the peaty-brown water and thrashing against the yielding scum beneath.

All morning the colonel rode ahead, stiff and formal on top of his stallion, but toward noon, he reined in and allowed Anson to catch up, stilling the cadence of his drum with a sign.

"Anson"—it was the first time his father had called him by name since he had become a Fencible—"this is the life of a Fencible. Not so grand as going into battle, I'll grant, but marching across country on the king's business. It's the life the men of our family have lived for generations. It's the life you'll lead yourself, and your son after you."

Anson nodded. "Yes, sir." To be among these Fencibles, to wear the red coat, it was all a boy could want—save carrying the musket. "Is there to be fighting, sir?"

The colonel shook his head. "None that I can see, more's the pity. Lord Melville—he is lately over, you know, to tend to his estates—Lord Melville has sent a simple task. Just past his demesne, hardly another hour's march from here, an outlaw keeps a valuable horse from His Lordship—this when the king's law is known plainly, that no Irishman may own a horse of value. We're to remind this fellow of that law."

"One man, then."

"One man, yes, but more than one man. All Ireland watches the king's arms. Let one man flout the law, and there will be such a loosening of the king's power that it will never be tightened again without blood. Swine will fly and roosters lay eggs before I'll let that happen." He looked behind him. "To the beat again, boy. We lag."

Anson could not help but be disappointed. Outlaws were just a little shy of pirates, and somehow this one man did not seem such a terrible villain. Still, if he threatened to send all Ireland into revolt . . .

At noon, the Fencibles broke for mess just outside a very small, very still town. When they re-formed and marched down into it, they passed huddling walls that bounded quiet, shuttered houses. At the far end of the town, they crossed a narrow stone bridge that arched sleekly over a dry riverbed. They paused by a nettle-covered graveyard to load cartridges, to give flanking squads their orders, and to rest a moment before they came upon the outlaw, whose lair lay just beyond the hillocky ground ahead.

Before the hedgerows began again, the flankers moved

to the north and south of the road, then pushed on, the rest of the regiment following. Anson felt the excitement tighten his stomach again. He was surprised, so intent was he on the drum roll and the coming encounter, that he noticed with startling clarity the pink hawthorn blossoms scattered in the hedges.

A last rise in the road, then the hedges spread out, and Anson was looking down at a cottage squatting in a vale beneath them, built close to the ground against the winter winds. Its thatching, grayed and ragged at the edges, was held down by a network of boulders, taken no doubt from the surrounding fields, where they grew like a crop. Hens and ducks cackled and waddled around the bare yard in front of the house, and a small group of hawthorn bushes held a row of shirts out to the sun, their arms spread as if in petition. Two goats circled a stake by a small dunghill. They looked nervously at the Fencibles, their bleating the only sound that Anson heard.

The marshy ground around the farm was all ablossom with white fly orchids and blue milkwort, and wild ferns unfurled their fronds to bob in the breeze that seeped down to the vale. A patch of yellow butterwort sprouted by the dairy, and rose vines, not yet flowered, climbed toward the vaulted roofs of the outbuildings. Smoke powdered the air above the chimney, and Anson sniffed at the earthy scent of burning peat. He had a sudden urge to sit quietly by the fire in that house.

"God's body, boy, are you about your duty or are you not?" Lieutenant Brockle stood by his side, scowling. Startled, Anson beat the march, and the Fencibles descended the vale, trampling the orchids and milkwort, reordering the landscape with their perfect lines and their perfect stepping. By the time they reached the farmhouse and frightened the goats into silence, the flankers had formed around the back and knelt in lines, muskets at the ready.

Silence. The breeze drew across the Fencible lines, and a horse nickered in the barn past the house. The colonel looked once at Lieutenant Brockle.

"Arthur Leary!" the lieutenant shouted. "Arthur Leary. You are declared outlaw. Yield yourself."

Longer silence. Anson swallowed and licked his lips.

Another nicker, and then a door swung savagely open and crashed back against the barn wall. A farmer limped haltingly out, leading a prince of a gelding, who walked with prancing steps. The horse's eyes were big and wide, and his tail arched. Slowly they made their way toward the farmhouse, their eyes fastened on the soldiers. "O'Leary," the farmer said, his voice stern with anger. "The name is Arthur O'Leary. And who is it that I'm to be yielding myself to?"

"The Staffordshire Fencibles."

"Thieves and cutthroats," he hollered back. "Thieves and cutthroats."

"No, sir. The king's own arm," returned the colonel.

"The king's own arm, is it?" shouted Arthur O'Leary, and he led the horse until he stood not fifteen paces from the Fencibles. "The king's own arm I myself have been, and it was as the king's own arm that I took a bullet below this knee. And it was as the king's own arm that I rode more charges than this boy has seen months in his life." He pointed to Anson, his hand quivering.

"The king's law . . ."

"I'll not be yielding a horse that saved my life time and again just on the whim of a mealy Londontown lord. A mealy lord with a stableful to carry his fat arse."

Lieutentant Brockle took a step forward and put his hand to his sword. "No Irishman may own a horse of value. It is the law."

"It is a damnable law, conceived by demons and registered in hell. I'll not be obeying it."

"Then you are an outlaw by your own admission." Lieutenant Brockle motioned to the Fencibles, and muskets came up to shoulders and aimed themselves at the outlaw.

"An outlaw by my own admission," said Arthur O'Leary, shaking his head. "An outlaw by my own admission. The Holy Mother herself is witness that I have never been anything but loyal to the king. But I'll tell you this: What you do now is but wickedly done. I'll not be giving up this horse to any lord. I'll not."

"Enough," said the colonel, standing in his stirrups.

"Lord Melville offered a fair price." At this, Arthur O'Leary spat upon the ground, but the colonel ignored him. "Yield the horse, and the business will be at an end."

Lieutentant Brockle, startled, turned back to the colonel. "Sir, he is a declared outlaw."

"Yield the horse," repeated the colonel.

But Arthur O'Leary would have none of it. Twirling his hand around the reins, he drew the horse's head down to him and kissed him on the nose. He pressed his forehead against the long muzzle, then stepped quickly back and drew a pistol from the inside of his jacket.

Time stopped, so that a moment was no different from a century, and in that moment the world exploded.

Arthur O'Leary leveled his pistol at the horse's head— or perhaps he was pointing beyond and leveling at Lieutenant Brockle.

Lieutenant Brockle drew his pistol.

The colonel shouted and spurred his horse forward.

The door to the farmhouse sprang open and a young O'Leary spurted out, an ancient musket aimed at the colonel.

An even younger O'Leary, no older than Anson himself, rushed to the door and was pulled back by his shrieking sister. "Leave me go, Sorcha," he screamed.

A shot from the ancient musket. Arthur O'Leary looked away from the horse. An explosion. Blue smoke covered the Fencibles.

And the goats began to bleat again at the death that was in their yard.

Anson heard himself yelling, not sure whether he was yelling at the colonel, at Lieutenant Brockle, at the Fencibles, or at the O'Learys. Maybe he was yelling at all the world that had begun to spin again and rush forward faster than he could hold it.

Another shriek, and the girl rushed out from the doorway. She stood between the bodies of her father and brother, looking from one to the other, her eyes as wild as the horse's, her hands dragging into her hair. Anson noticed that the breeze had stopped and the blue smoke still hovered around the Fencibles as she knelt by the side of her father, holding his head and stroking his face. The only sound in the yard was the bleating of the goats and her low moan.

The youngest O'Leary came and stood by the side of his brother. He bent down to pick up the gun, and Anson knew that if he had had powder and shot, he would have fired it off at the Fencibles. Instead, he stood holding the gun across his chest and staring down at his brother. When he looked up, his eyes met Anson's.

And suddenly Anson was ashamed. He was a Staffordshire Fencible. He wore the red coat of the king's own realm. He had come to Ireland to defend His Majesty. And here was the youngest O'Leary, standing ragged in front of a low cottage. His father had been declared outlaw.

His father threatened the king's peace. The Fencibles had defended that peace.

But still the youngest O'Leary stared at Anson, and his blue eyes accused.

Lieutenant Brockle strode across the yard, still holding his pistol. The reins of the horse were looped around the dead man's hand and he had trouble freeing them, but with a jerk he pulled them out. Leading the horse, he brought it to the colonel. "For Lord Melville, sir. There looks to be not a single scratch on him. Every shot must have been true."

The colonel did not move. His eyes were on the girl in front of him.

"Shall I pay her the fee that Lord Melville sent, sir? We've no obligation, of course, as he was a declared outlaw."

The colonel turned to look at Lieutenant Brockle. "No obligation, Lieutenant?" He paused. "Pay her the fee. God knows she'll need it now. Pay her the fee."

Lieutenant Brockle took a pouch from the colonel's saddlebags and handed it to Anson. "Mr. Staplyton, perhaps she would understand the spirit in which this is meant if you were to take it to her."

"Yes, sir." Anson unslung the drum from his shoulder and walked slowly into the yard. Behind him he could hear Lieutenant Brockle organizing the regiment for its return. Ahead of him he knew that the youngest O'Leary was staring at him with all the hatred of the world in his soul.

He stood before the girl. She did not look up.

"Your servant, ma'am," said Anson, a little unsteadily, holding out the pouch. "Lord Melville wishes to extend payment for the horse." For a long time she gave no answer. She was still, holding her father as close to her as she could.

"Ma'am," said Anson quietly, "you will need this."

Then the youngest O'Leary sprinted over and snatched the pouch from Anson's hand. His face showed the scouring of tears, and his black hair was damp with sweat. With one hand he gripped the pouch, squeezing it tight. The other he thrust out at Anson, and it was bloody.

"I wear the red too," he shouted. "Only my red has more glory and honor in it than yours ever will. It is my brother's blood, Fencible. Do you understand? My brother's blood." He ripped the pouch open, shook the sovereigns into his bloodied hand, and threw them at Anson, who ducked as they struck him.

"Would God that they were shot," he yelled. "Would God that they were. Then we would show the Fencibles work that was bravely done. Would God that they were shot."

Anson put his hand to his cheek where one of the sovereigns had struck, and when he took it away, he found that there was blood on his fingers. "He was a declared outlaw," he said weakly.

"He was a farmer," answered the youngest O'Leary, and suddenly the recognition of his father's death overwhelmed him like the sea. Anson watched him crumple into himself, watched his knees buckle, watched him fall down into his sister's arms. They rocked back and forth, holding each other so tightly that their fingers were white.

Anson stared at them until Lieutenant Brockle called.

The regiment behind him had re-formed, and Anson returned to its head, behind the colonel. Lieutenant Brockle held the horse.

"Shall I collect the sovereigns and have the horse taken to Lord Melville, sir? Excuse me, sir, shall I have the horse taken to Lord Melville?"

"Mr. Brockle, you may have the horse taken to hell, for all I care."

The lieutenant stepped back as if struck. "He was a declared outlaw, sir. The king's law is clear on this matter."

The colonel waved him off. "Take a squad and do what you must. Be back to New Barracks by nightfall. See to it that you are no later. Mr. Staplyton, beat to the march. Mr. Staplyton!"

But Anson had not heard. He had turned back to the low vale, where everything seemed so much as it had been when they had first arrived. Even the shirts were still drying on the hawthorn bushes. But now, there was a girl and young boy struggling between them to carry the body of their father into the house, and passing the body of their brother. Anson shook his head in wonder. How could it be that death—Death—had come so suddenly, when he was hardly watching?

"God's wounds, Mr. Staplyton! Beat to the march!"

Anson started back into awareness, and his hands automatically beat out the rhythm. They climbed up the way they had come, crushing fly orchids and ferns.

None of the Fencibles spoke of the events of the day after evening mess. The songs they sang while gathered around the coal stove, the stories of home, the old laughs that grew better as they grew older—none of these came. Anson went to bed in stillness. He was surprised to find himself thinking so much of his mother and sisters, of the day he had first put on the red coat, of the glorious tales of his grandfather.

He put his hand to his cheek and found it wet.

# CHAPTER

## 3

"*H*e threw the sovereigns in young Staplyton's face, did he? Threw them in his face? Swine. Popish, arrogant swine. Did I not tell you, Staplyton? Did I not tell you they were swine?"

"You did, my lord." The colonel inclined his head humbly.

"The most deuced thing. I offer the man fair payment under the law for a horse far grander than any he should need to cart his peat—far grander—and the man refuses me. Refuses me with the most abominable language. Have you ever heard the like, young Staplyton?"

"No, sir."

"Or you, Corporal Oakes? Have you ever heard such impudence?"

"Impudence is the word, my lord."

"And the sovereigns?"

"I have them here, my lord," assured Lieutenant Brockle.

Lord Melville shook his head. "I tell you, Colonel"—and here he raised a glass of dark Madeira—"I tell you, the Irish are a sodden, lazy people, who will find the least excuse to tweak the king's nose. It makes a man sleep better in his bed, knowing that the Staffordshire Fencibles are in New Barracks to check their barbarism. Imagine, he threw the sovereigns in young Staplyton's face. And what did you reply, man?"

Anson felt that he ought to have replied something clever, but all he remembered was the shame of the moment. "I replied nothing, sir," he said.

"Nothing? Had it been me, a score and ten younger, had it been me, I would have knocked the beggar in the dust by his outlaw father's side. In the dust, I say."

"Having completed our duty, it was undoubtedly wise to withdraw," said the colonel evenly.

Lord Melville stared for a moment at the colonel, then nodded his head and smiled. "Undoubtedly. And the result of it all is that a fine gelding stands in my stables, and you stand in my hall as my guests. By God, Colonel, Ireland has led me to a perfect pitch of melancholy, what with its want of company and the vapors of its boggy situation. Lieutenant Fielding, you yourself look rather palsied."

"Only a crimp in my stomach, my lord."

"Lieutenant Brockle has no crimp."

"Some men, my lord, have stronger stomachs than others."

A cough from the colonel. "My lord, before we sup, you would favor us with a tour of your demesne?"

Lord Melville finished a gulp of his Madeira. "I will. I will indeed. I think you shall find, Colonel, elegance on a scale you will seldom see outside the king's England." And with a grand wave of his arm, Lord Melville led his guests across the hall to the glass doors held open by two perfectly matched and powdered footmen.

Anson was the last to leave, and he listened to the echo of his footsteps on the tiles of the floor—Italian marble, Lord Melville had pointed out. The cooler air from outside chilled him, but he put his face up to it with delight after the overheated hall. He shivered with pleasure and wished suddenly that he were back in Gadshall on a cool spring afternoon. He wondered if his father ever wished for the same thing.

Just this morning he had spoken to the colonel for the first time since their expedition four days past. The colonel's eyes had been searching when he came into his quarters.

"Drummer, there is an invitation from Lord Melville to dinner. A kind of celebration, he says. He invites all the officers and you, especially. He writes that he is most eager to meet my son."

"Yes, sir." Anson's voice came low and quiet.

A long pause. "You are not pleased by the invitation?"

"No, sir."

"I see. Doubtless you refer to the affair of the gelding."

"Sir, two men are dead for no reason other than Lord Melville's desire for a horse."

"Boy, you speak to your colonel."

"My apologies, sir."

The colonel paced twice across the room, his hands grasped behind his back. "Lord Melville was within his rights. If the fellow . . . Damnation, this need not have happened."

Silence draped between them. The sounds of the muster came in from the quadrangle, and both father and son turned to the window to watch.

"There is," the Colonel began, then stopped. Another silence. "There is," he began again, "a certain way of life in His Majesty's service. In the Fencibles. It is a life of duty and service, yes. But promotions are hard to come by, most particularly in a time of relative peace. You do understand this, boy?"

"I understand, sir."

"To rise in the king's Fencibles, one must have the backing of one close to the king's ear, a patron, if you will. The families of Lord Melville and the Staplytons have been attached in such patronage for generations. You understand that too."

"I do."

Colonel Staplyton rose and paced to the window, and for a moment as the morning sunlight silhouetted his face, Anson saw himself grown older. He did not know that the colonel, looking at him, had seen the reverse.

"You will be Lord Melville's guest at his demesne this afternoon. Parade dress."

"I will be ready, sir."

"You will. Dismissed."

Now, as he stood at the glass doors, the footmen waiting to close them behind him, Anson pondered the lost moment. He wished that the colonel had said something more, but he did not know what.

Lord Melville strode like a god through the grounds of his demesne. "Mark this urn, Staplyton. You'll see one at each turn of the path. All from Italy, mind you. And there, past those hedges—no, no, there, Staplyton, where Lieutenant Fielding gazes—that parapet is for my pigeons. Do you mark how they strut, Corporal Oakes?"

"I mark the strutting, sir,"

"You'll see none finer."

"Indeed, sir." Corporal Oakes turned to Anson and whispered, "It wasn't the strutting of the pigeons I was marking," and Anson had to choke his sudden guffaw into a pretended cough.

Had Lord Melville not bullied them along, Anson knew that he would have been entranced by the place. Lines of hedges ran out from the central path, each leading gracefully to gardens of roses not yet bloomed, but with glossy green leaves heralding sweet flowers. Then the path opened out to a meadow of apple and cherry trees, each pruned to a perfect roundness, each treading in rich, dark soil that circled out to a perfect trim of grass. Blossoms lay upon the branches like new snow, and the heaviness of their perfume was like liquor. Other than their feet on the gravel and the bluster of Lord Melville, the only sound was that of bees, who buzzed so loudly that even Lord Melville had to shout.

"This was all farmland once. Imagine it. Farmland. There is no eye for beauty in this country. None at all."

"The fruit must be abundant, sir," pointed out Lieutenant Brockle.

"Abundant?" Lord Melville waved his hand grandly in dismissal. "I know nothing of that. The trees are raised for their flowers, and you are fortunate enough to see them just at their height. Another week and they will be less. Another day, even."

"They are without peer," said the colonel.

"Even so. Now gentlemen, let me direct you to the canal. This was bogland when I came, cut to pieces for its peat. Cut to pieces. I had the bottom of the canal cleared and the water directed anew. A stand of old willows drooped over it, and I had them all cut down and those new aspens planted. You'll mark how they flourish."

The company marked their flourishing.

"The canal I have stocked with trout and eel. Of the

45

two, the latter puts up the better fight, but the former is by far the better tasting. Mark, there, how one jumps."

But Anson was tired of marking. He let the company drift ahead of him, and when they rounded a turn, he continued another way, hidden by higher hedges. Another turn down an avenue of old yews, and he had lost them completely in the cool, scented darkness. He paused to allow the silence to settle its hands on him and then walked slowly between the grand trees, letting the soft needles of their branches waft against his face.

The sound of water came to Anson at the end of the yews, and he followed it to a bank of holly that bent along a deep, fast stream. A break in it let him down to the water. He pushed both hands in, shocked by the cold, and splashed the water to his face.

Then he saw the salmon. Dozens, scores of them, their bodies thick as paving stones, filling the river and crowding it so that it turned red with their scales. Their high fins creased the water and churned it white as they rushed upstream, rushing to the one thing that they must do, rushing where they must against all hope. Anson watched them for a long, long time.

It was late afternoon before Anson came back to the manor house, finding the colonel pacing impatiently. "Mr. Staplyton," he began.

"Young Staplyton," called Lord Melville, "we feared we had lost you among the hedgerows."

"You had not, sir. I was enjoying the river that runs through your gardens."

"A splendid river, is it not? I had it diverted to its present course and stock it with salmon each spring. They begin their run about this time, I believe."

"They have indeed begun, sir." The river had suddenly become less.

"Even so. But had you been a minute later, you would have delayed us."

"I would have regretted it, sir."

"And you would have missed the hunt—not that it will be a grand, regal hunt, such as we might have in England. But step into the stable, boy."

"A hunt, my lord? With pleasure!" And it was with real pleasure that Anson stepped into the stables—a groom was already waiting with his mount—and returned astride a russet mare who barely held back her eagerness for the open run. Anson could barely hold himself back.

He looked toward the colonel and grinned. Anson knew that his father was not a handsome man, but on the back of a horse, he was a sight of beauty. He rode like a jockey, low to the neck, his legs tight and high. And the speed! Why, his father could climb on an old carthorse and it would run like Pegasus, just for him.

Grooms held horses for the rest of the Fencible guests. The hooves clattered against the cobbled stones, echoing against the whitewashed walls of the stables. When the dogs were loosed, they bayed their tones to the air, and their clamoring and scattering scurried the martins out of the nests they had built under the roof tiles. Two grooms bundled Lord Melville up onto his new gelding, and with a quick turn they all roared out under an arched gate into the countryside, following the pack of long-eared dogs, whose curling tails bobbed up and down with their frantic running.

Down the gravel road that circled the front of the manor house, through the long hedgerow that stood between the demesne and a lane, into a patch of young wood, and then across a just-plowed field, the horses churning the furrows into a chaos of mud. Hounds and Fencibles chased Lord Melville, whose "Hallo, Hallo!" came back to them carrying raucous pleasure. There was no need to urge the mare. Faster and faster they rode, and Anson heard himself echoing Lord Melville's call. In a whirlwind of speed, they blurred fences. Sheep and goats rasping at the grass raised their heads at their passing, and an old horse remembered its glory days and whinnied dangerously to the air.

Several times Anson pushed himself up in his stirrups to see his father ride. He must have far outstripped them all. He must certainly have ridden past Lord Melville, whose clumpy awkwardness made his gelding throw his head back and forth and shy from one side to the other. But whenever Anson looked, he saw his father well back from Lord Melville, sitting high and holding the reins tight. Once he saw his father pull back sharply when his mount began to outpace the gelding.

It was to be a disappointing afternoon, and not just for Anson.

"I could almost believe that every fox in the county has got wind of us and run to den. Damn and blast."

"Lord Melville," suggested the colonel, "sometimes a fox can trick the very best dogs in all the world."

"Not these dogs. Not a one. It must simply be too early in the spring in this backward country."

"Undoubtedly."

They stopped at a small rivulet that coursed between banks pillowed by the softest, greenest moss. The dogs rushed and plunged their muzzles in, coming up with water in their noses, shaking the spray and flapping their ears before they plunged in again. The horses stepped delicately through the moss and into the streambed, lowering their heads elegantly and with dignity, and then flopping the water into their mouths just as fast as the dogs.

Anson dismounted to let his mare drink and stood at her side, stroking her. Across the water, a songbird trilled, and when Anson turned to follow it, he saw a stone cross. It cropped out of the high grass, long and tall. Though the Irish wet had weathered it for years beyond all memory, Anson could still make out the lacy patterns that wove in and out and around, and the simple circle that topped it all.

Against the frippery of the hunt, the cold gray stone seemed eternal.

Lord Melville was pointing the stone out to the colonel. "Not the best of examples, but still, a moderately good hand. Moderately good. I've passed this way and seen it covered with flowers, left by some ignorant soul praying for a harvest, no doubt. I believe I shall have it dug up and removed to my gardens within the fortnight. I imagine the stone covered with roses, or perhaps set at the very head of the lane—though there it will need something to soften it. It seems too hard."

"Perhaps nasturtiums, my lord."

"The very thing, Lieutenant Brockle. The very thing."

"But my lord," said Lieutenant Fielding slowly, "the cross has stood here for hundreds of years."

"Over a thousand, I should say."

"A thousand then, my lord. It hardly seems right to remove something that has weathered so very well, and that the people hereabouts still come to, just as their families have come for generation after generation."

"Popish nonsense, Lieutenant Fielding. Popish nonsense. It is not for us to encourage that sort of thing. Not at all. Do you for a moment believe that placing flowers atop a cross will bring in a harvest?"

"But my lord, the flowers are hardly the point. The stone has been there for so long—"

"I disagree, Lieutenant. The flowers are precisely the

point. What are we about in this forsaken place if not to bring it to a new order?"

"Just so, my lord, yet—"

"A new order, I say. That is why boys such as young Staplyton here join His Majesty's service. To extend His Majesty's dominion over all the world, not to encourage superstitious claptrap. Do you not agree, young Staplyton?"

By now the dogs had finished lapping and were sprinting, noses to the ground, all about them. The horses turned to the banks, peacefully pulling at tufts and tossing their manes. As the moments passed, Anson felt the weight of betrayal.

"My lord," said Lieutenant Fielding, "I withdraw my observation. Such a cross only encourages what should long ago have ended."

"Just so, just so," said Lord Melville, his good humor restored. "And now, gentlemen, we have a supper awaiting us. I think you will find the duckling of the best."

The colonel turned with Lord Melville up the bank, but before Lieutenant Fielding followed, his eyes met Anson's. "My thanks to you, sir," said Anson. The lieutenant nodded and rode on. As the dogs rushed ahead, Anson set his foot to the stirrup to mount, and then stopped. He looked about him and found a patch of purple violets run riot against the green moss. He plucked them quickly, almost savagely, waded across the stream, and arranged them on top of the stone. Then he hurried to his horse.

The duckling at supper was of the best, as was everything else in Lord Melville's manor. They sat at a table whose delicate legs curved gracefully to the floor, and ate from scalloped jasperware and porcelain plates that caught the reflection from the table's glossy wood. Bright silver candelabra held a host of candles, and above the table a chandelier imprisoned the light in dripping glass.

Lord Melville was the happiest of hosts and paid special attention to Anson. "Ah, the pudding. You must try the pudding, young Staplyton. No, not enough at all. You must fill your platter at the least. At the least, I say. You'll not find food such as this at New Barracks."

"No indeed, sir," Anson agreed, and with the warmth of the room and the heaviness of the food, Anson felt himself enjoying this world, regretting the business of the stone cross as plain foolishness, and thinking that it was, after all, grand to have a patron and to be a Staffordshire Fencible.

"If only I had a son such as yours, Staplyton," called Lord Melville across the table.

"You have no children, my lord?" asked Lieutenant Brockle.

"Nor a wife. I have had no time for such folderol."

"But are you not lonely at times, sir?" asked Lieutenant Fielding.

Lord Melville looked up sharply. "Lonely?" he asked. "Lonely? A lord need never be lonely, Lieutenant."

"Then if not lonely, sir, do you not miss seeing a son

grow in the ways of this world, seeing him move past childhood and on into manhood?"

Lord Melville silently considered the bottom of his wineglass for a moment. Then he looked up quickly and answered, Anson thought, almost too jovially. "I do not. To have children about the place, with all their mewling and screeching. No, no. Let them be hatched fully grown, and then I would think of it. Gentlemen, consider the smells!"

At this, all the Fencibles laughed. But Anson saw that Lord Melville watched him and did not laugh.

The dinner ended with port and toasts to His Majesty's good health. Lord Melville pushed his chair back and spread his hands over his belly. "Gentleman, music in the garden. There's a quartet of mine that is more than passable."

"My lord, we must soon be back at New Barracks, else we would be pleased—"

"Nonsense, Colonel. We must all have some entertainment among ourselves in this desolate part of the world. But if it is not to be music . . ." He hesitated a moment, and then his face broke into delight. "Swords it is. Surely a Fencible will not disdain a parry or two. You, Colonel, would you cross a sword with me?"

The colonel hesitated, looked for a moment at Anson, then nodded. "As you wish, my lord," and at Lord Melville's clap, wigged servants appeared to whisk away the plates and to clear a lane down one side of the drawing room.

"My lord, may I offer you my sword?" said Lieutenant Brockle.

"Most handsome, Lieutenant." Lord Melville took up his stance against the colonel.

Anson smiled at what he knew must come. He had fenced against his father too often to doubt that he would easily outmatch Lord Melville.

Anson watched the quick, lithe hands of the colonel and waited for the subtle, almost undetectable movement that would slap a sword from the palm of an opponent. Lord Melville's first thrusts showed that the colonel would need do little more than parry. When the colonel passed by two, then three, then four easy marks, Anson's smile grew even broader.

But then, Anson saw the colonel spread open his stance, stiffen his knees, and turn face on. His elbow dropped slightly. With a cry, Lord Melville rushed in, slapped the sword from the colonel's hand, and laid his point against the colonel's chest. "Staplyton, you have never conceived that one maneuver."

"I never have, my lord. I have no defense against it."

"It is the preliminary feint, Staplyton, that you must watch. But another pass. Come."

The colonel picked up his sword again. "My lord—"

"Come, Staplyton. I insist upon it."

The colonel did not look at Anson. He squared his

shoulders and held his sword point up. "I shall guard against that maneuver, my lord."

"Little good will it do you," and Lord Melville began his wild thrusting again.

This time the colonel kept his guard, but backed and backed. Once or twice he pressed his opponent, but when Lord Melville retreated in grunting surprise, the colonel paused as if for breath, and Lord Melville came to the attack again. Finally, he charged with a series of awkward, brutish thrusts raining down from above, leaving his belly and chest open for the colonel to attack. But he never did, and the rains of blows ended in Lord Melville's triumphant call of "Yield," which the colonel did.

"Well done, my lord, well done. Mastery achieved by elegance mixed with force."

"Just so, Lieutenant Brockle. Just so."

"And now, my lord," began the colonel.

"And now having defeated the father, it seems that I must turn to the son."

The colonel glanced quickly at Anson, and Anson saw something he had never seen in his father's eyes. It was something he knew had been in his own eyes just four days ago, at the O'Leary cottage.

"My lord," said the colonel, "he is hardly a fit subject for your fencing. He is—"

"He is a Fencible, Colonel Staplyton, and wise in the

ways of this world, without a doubt. He should make a good accounting of himself. Is it not so, young Staplyton?"

Anson paused a moment and turned to his father. But his father said nothing. Now his face gave no clue.

"It is so, my lord," said Anson. "If I might borrow Corporal Oakes's sword?"

"Come, Oakes," said Lord Melville. "Quickly, man."

Corporal Oakes unbuckled his sword and came to Anson, strapping it around his waist.

"Anson," he whispered, "even a fat man can move quickly, and he will use his weight to advantage."

"Come, come," urged Lord Melville. "Such strategizing is hardly the mark of a Fencible."

"And he will not be pleased to lose," rushed Colonel Oakes.

"I understand, sir," said Anson.

Corporal Oakes nodded, then winked.

"He takes his stance well, Colonel, this cub of yours."

"Indeed, my lord."

"And he parries well. Good, young Staplyton. Good. You take the thrust admirably. But perhaps you have not seen maneuvers such as these before." With a feint of his head, he rushed at Anson's palm—a rush that Anson shoved aside with only a slight turn of his wrist, declining at the last moment to take the advantage that lay open to him.

Lord Melville was not pleased. "That was a maneuver your father was never able to master."

"Good fortune alone saved me, sir."

Lord Melville grunted and returned to the attack. But as Anson parried, parried, parried, Lord Melville's thrusts became slashes that whipped the air to a frenzy about them.

"The most deuced thing," he said, stepping back. "It must be the bend of your sword, Brockle. It has too much give in it."

"A thousand pardons, my lord. I have often thought so myself."

"Is it in the hilt, Brockle?" he asked, holding it out for the lieutenant to examine.

"Perhaps, my lord, the problem lies with—" But he never finished his sentence. Anson had dropped his guard when Lord Melville turned to Lieutenant Brockle, and suddenly Lord Melville wheeled about so that the point of his sword slashed across the top of Anson's cheekbone, leaving a curtain of blood.

With a cry, Corporal Oakes leaped between them, whisking out a handkerchief to cover the wound. He glared at the colonel, but when the colonel remained still, Oakes turned to Lord Melville.

"Foul! A foul trick that no gentleman—"

"Colonel," said Lord Melville evenly, "this puppy yaps."

"And yap he might!" yelled Oakes.

"Corporal, you are dismissed," called Colonel Staplyton sharply. "You will wait outside. No, you will say no more."

Corporal Oakes turned back to Anson. "Hold the

kerchief here. Yes, just so. That will stanch the blood. When we get back to New Barracks—"

"Dismissed, Corporal!"

Oakes strode out of the room without looking at Lord Melville, who leaned back on the bend of his sword.

"The hilt, Lieutenant Brockle, seems not to be a problem after all. Young Staplyton, you must remember to keep the elbow up. Up like this. And angle your body to present the smaller target. Like so. You see?"

"Lord Melville," began the colonel.

"Yes, of course, Colonel, you must be heading back, and I have a quartet to attend to. You have given me a most diverting afternoon. I shall look forward to another." And as the colonel bowed, Lord Melville handed the sword to Lieutenant Brockle and passed out the garden doors.

# 4

$\mathcal{A}$nson woke the next morning with his hand pressed against his stitched and throbbing face. He looked up to see a dark, wet ceiling. Whoever fixed the roof must be a better Fencible than he is a carpenter, he thought, and then curled out of the way as a drop formed and quivered above him.

He dressed in the dank cold, a cold that grew danker as he drummed to the muster outside, and danker as the colonel inspected, and even danker as Lieutenant Fielding put the regiment through its wheeling and facing.

"God's death, gentlemen, you march like a line of laundry women. Your backs straight. Straight. Straight, by the mothers that bore you, you unnatural whips!" Lieutenant Fielding was in a foul temper.

The weather put everyone in a foul temper, so there were squalls during the mess. The Fencibles were packed side by side on the benches, the smell of their wet uniforms stronger even than the dried beef and porridge. Corporal

Oakes sat at the end of the table, his face a storm, and at the high table at the front of the room, Lieutenant Fielding scowled so severely that no one would sit beside him.

The story of Anson's stitches had crossed the regiment, and whenever a Fencible walked behind him, he would thump Anson on the shoulder.

"Just a bit of blood."

"You'll look like a pirate with that."

"As fierce as Bloody Captain Morgan himself."

Anson did not hear what the Fencibles said of Lord Melville, or their oaths to let him fetch his own misbegotten horse the next time.

Lieutenant Fielding rose to dismiss the mess, and the Fencibles filed out into the dank and back to their patrols. But Corporal Oakes grabbed Anson by the elbow, shouting above the scraping of benches and clattering of boots on the wooden floor. "We're to see the lieutenant."

"Sir?"

"An assignment brought in this morning. From Lord Melville." Anson nodded, and together they pushed through the soldiers to the high table.

Lieutenant Fielding greeted them with a small nod. "Dr. Hoccleve's stitches are small and neat, Drummer. I suppose there will hardly be a scar."

"Yes, sir. It is nothing at all, sir."

"Hardly nothing at all had it been three quarters of an inch higher. But to the assignment." He coughed once, twice. "Lord Melville regrets that payment was never made for his horse. He wishes the Fencibles to deliver ten sovereigns to the surviving family, with his compliments. He requests specifically that you, Corporal Oakes, and you, Drummer, carry out his request. Afterward, he invites you to his demesne where he promises to serve a brace of the finest ducks for your supper." Lieutenant Fielding cleared his throat again. "I believe, gentlemen, that Lord Melville means this assignment by way of apology."

Corporal Oakes clenched and unclenched his hands. His mouth twisted.

"Yes, sir," said Anson. "Are we to leave at once?"

"At once. The corporal has already received the sovereigns. And Corporal, in accepting Lord Melville's invitation to dine, you are also promising to remember the dignity of your rank and position."

A long moment, during which Lieutenant Fielding eyed the corporal evenly.

"Indeed, sir."

It was not until they had packed their kits, chosen mounts, and were well past the gates to New Barracks that Corporal Oakes broke out with a string of curses so pungent that mothers in upstairs apartments clapped their hands to their children's ears, and curs that had been kicked and beshouted all their lives scurried away with tails curved beneath them.

"Damn and blast the man. Damn and blast him. Does

he believe a brace of ducks sufficient reparation? A brace of ducks? Let him choke on his scrawny, bony ducks. By God, let him—"

"Sir," interrupted Anson, "I'm sure that they will be the finest that are to be had in this desolate country."

At this, the storm evaporated from Corporal Oakes's face and he grinned into laughter. He dropped his voice an octave. "The finest to be had this side of London. Indeed, sir, this side of the equator itself."

And laughing, they rode past Phoenix Park and out into the countryside.

The mist around them pinked, then yellowed, then whitened, until suddenly they found themselves riding beneath a bright blue sky.

"There are two occasions when it is best to be a Fencible," said Oakes. "The first is when you are in the smoke of battle and the cannon are gouging the air overhead. And the second is when you are on detached assignment, with no lieutenant eyeing you, and you can jump into a stream like that one just there, or lie down in a bank of heather, or dawdle the afternoon away in the sun."

"Though we've the sovereigns to deliver."

Oakes reined in his horse and sat, grinning. "Anson," he said, "bother the sovereigns. We'll deliver them soon enough and have more time than we want to get to the brace of ducks. There's more to life than drill and patrol, drill and patrol, wheel and face, wheel and face."

"I know that."

"Do you now?" And suddenly Oakes leaned over and pushed Anson from astride the horse, so that he landed on his back in the dust of the road. Oakes jumped down beside him. "A race to the top of that rise. See if your younger legs can carry you past me!"

They almost could, but Corporal Oakes kept one or two strides ahead the whole way up. Then they stood together, panting and laughing, as the whole of Ireland stretched out before their eyes. Meadow after meadow patched the land-scape together like a quilt, seamed with hedgerows and bespeckled with buttercups and dandelions, foxgloves and meadowsweets. They knelt and watched the run of the breeze across it, the smell of crushed mint and lavender rising around them.

"Not such a desolate country after all," murmured Anson.

Oakes nodded. "You see it then. You see it. We imagine Ireland as hardly more than a bog we've come to put to rights. But what if it does not need to be put to rights?"

"The king decides what is right," said Anson.

"What he decides on his throne in London is one thing. But Anson, if the king were sitting here seeing this, would he decide the same thing?"

Anson looked out at the soft green mirror of the land, shadowed by the clouds that hung aloft. "I wish that it could always be as it is," he answered.

"And that, you rebellious son of a colonel, is what most Irishmen say too."

They were silent a long while, and content to be silent as the panorama of the clouds blew across the green of Ireland. The place was wilder and deeper than Gadshall, older and more mysterious. It would not have been surprising if a line of druid priests had suddenly sprung up from the turf and begun their incantations.

"Well, young Staplyton," said Corporal Oakes finally, "we could stay up here most of the morning, except that your mount seems to be wandering away and promises you a long walk to New Barracks tonight." With a cry, Anson leaped up and raced after his mount. Oakes took one last look over the rise, then followed.

By the time they reached the cottage, the sun had passed its height and was throwing long shadows. The yard below was quiet and still, the goats no longer tied up—perhaps they hid in the barn. It was as it had been before, but less abundant, less full of life, more wary. They rode down quietly.

"You think there will be anyone there?" asked Anson.

"They'll be there."

"They will not be pleased to see us."

"No, they will not. And that is one of the reasons Lord Melville himself decided not to come—not that he would bestir his fat self from his fat demesne to do so in any event."

Closer and still closer, and Anson could see that there had been a change. Peat stacks were mounded up against the side of the barn, enough peat and more for next winter's fires. When he pointed them out, Oakes nodded. "It's what you do for a neighbor," he murmured. "It shames us."

Into the yard now, and they paused, Anson's horse whinnying with the wind. Oakes clambered down from his mount. Anson followed, then waited while Oakes found the ten sovereigns in his saddlebags. The pouch clinked in the quiet.

"Are there to be thirty pieces in it, then?" came a voice from the cottage, and when Anson looked, he saw the hedge master, Owen Roe Sullivan himself, standing in the doorway with his arms folded. Behind him, the boy who had thrown the sovereigns at Anson stood stiffly.

Oakes hesitated; then he crossed the yard, Anson holding the horses' halters. "Pride is all well and good," he said. "But when there is hunger in a house . . ."

"Are you the one to be telling an Irishman about hunger?"

A long silence. "No, I am not," said Oakes finally.

"No, you are not," repeated the hedge master. "God said that man would earn his bread by the sweat of his brow. But you English believe the divine curse not harsh enough. You deny even the means of sweat."

He turned to Anson. "And you, boyo. Have you ever eaten the rancid rinds of potatoes to keep your stomach at bay through the night? Or have you listened to the young ones in your house crying, and you nothing to give them to make them stop? Have you?" he asked fiercely.

"No, sir."

The hedge master held his hands up to his face. "First you come and take the land that we have farmed since St. Ciaran of blessed memory came back to Ireland. Then when that is not enough, you take what we grow, and then the means of our farming itself. And when even that is not enough, you take our lives." He closed his eyes and shook his head. "And now you come with sovereigns to pay us."

Anson stood with misted eyes, feeling as if the land itself, the very green of it, were attacking him in his bright-red Fencible coat. One of the horses whinnied softly, and Anson wished that he could stroke its mane.

"Sir," said Oakes, stepping forward with the pouch, "our assignment is to deliver this money to this family. Will you step aside and allow me to do that?"

The boy shouldered past the hedge master. "By the saints, you will come no nearer. The blood on your hands is my father's and my brother's, and you will come no nearer." He stooped and picked up a rock. "No nearer," he repeated savagely.

The hedge master took him by the elbow. "There has been enough of bloodletting in this yard," he said quietly. The boy's face tore at the words. Then, suddenly, a great sob heaved out of his chest and, bent nearly double, he ran past them into the barn. His sobbing came back to them, muffled.

"There is still the matter of the payment," said Oakes.

"Yes," the hedge master whispered. "Still the matter of the payment. But it is hardly my place to accept or refuse. For that, you must come inside and speak to the girl you have bereft. Tell me, sirs, have you ever once been inside an Irish house? Not the demesnes, but a real house of God-fearing Irish, whose hands have been building and working all their lives?"

They said nothing.

"I thought as much. Come and see what you have conquered," and he stood aside.

The inside of the cottage was dark, warmed only by the glowing peat fire in the hearth. The room was simple and contained all of the O'Learys' life. On one side, a long table spanned the width, hay chairs pulled up to it. A lamp hanging from a crossbeam lit its dark surface dully. In the corners past it, piles of cabbages and turnips heaped themselves one upon the other, held in place by barrels filled with potatoes. On the other side, another table supported a pile of battered books and scattered papers. The benches were thrown back from it, as though someone had leaped from the table and hustled up the stairs against the far wall. In front of those stairs, as if to protect them, stood the girl.

When Anson stooped into the cottage and looked at

her, he was surprised at what he saw. Her face did not show hatred; it showed fear. And Anson knew for the first time what it was to bring fear to another person. He almost began to fear himself.

"Sorcha," said the hedge master quietly, "there are two Fencibles who'll be seeing you." She said nothing. She did not move.

"Madam," said Oakes, "we have come to bring you some payment and to extend our deepest apologies for what has happened."

At this, the hedge master raised one eyebrow in surprise.

Oakes took the pouch and laid it on the table with the books and papers. The girl still did not move.

"I too wish to offer my apologies," said Anson. "Anything we can do . . ."

"Anything you can do," the girl repeated. "You offer anything that you can do after destroying more than you can repay."

"Ten sovereigns in such a time . . ." began Oakes.

But the girl was looking at Anson, and she saw his eye on the cottage. "Do you dare scorn and pity us? Do you dare? Sure, we are the richest people in the world. We have the faith. And what is it that you have? A stolen horse." She sat down at the table heavily, and it seemed as if she suddenly had grown weaker and smaller. Certainly her voice grew quieter. "Still, there is one thing you might do. You might be asking Lord Melville to leave us alone, now that he has done to us what he has done."

"Madam," said Oakes, "Lord Melville has no—"

"You haven't seen, have you? You haven't seen what happens when a tenant can no longer meet the rents a lord sets. Rents on land we once owned. Won't the day come when he sends his agents—or maybe even you—to cart us from our own land so he can hire a new, stronger farmer? Won't the day come?"

Anson looked at Oakes's face and saw that she was right. Just as sure as the tide, Lord Melville would demand his tenancy, and when this family could not pay its rent, he would evict them. Oakes had no doubt.

Anson unbuttoned his red coat in the heat of the house and said simply, "I will speak to Lord Melville. I will see to it."

But she only looked at him with scorn, as if she knew he could do nothing.

Corporal Oakes cleared his throat. "We're to be away now," he said.

The hedge master stepped forward and took Anson by the shoulders, peering deeply into his face. "I believe you will do as you say," he said softly. "The Lord himself knows how this house depends upon it."

"We will not depend upon the word of a Fencible," came the girl's voice. Her fear was gone now before the red anger that flushed her face. "No good ever came of that!"

"No," said the hedge master, without turning from Anson. "No good has ever come of that. But Sorcha, it is not for us to say that there will never be any good come of that." He paused, then said to Anson, "You will speak to Lord Melville?"

"I will, sir."

He nodded his head and released Anson's shoulders. "Perhaps that is enough for now. Even if Lord Melville were to refuse you, it is enough for now that a Fencible should undertake to do the asking."

Then he turned to Oakes. "And you, Corporal. What will you do? Will you report what you have seen here?" He waved his arm to the table.

In the silence that followed, Anson looked from Oakes to the hedge master, then back to Oakes. He did not understand the battle that he saw in Oakes's face. "Sir," said Anson, "there is nothing to report except our bringing of the payment."

"Is that so, Corporal?" asked the hedge master.

"If our regimental drummer says it is so, then it is so," replied Oakes. At this, Sorcha sighed deeply. When Anson looked at her, it seemed that she was about to cry.

"Drummer," said Oakes, "we have an engagement. Your servant, sir."

"We will not take the sovereigns," called Sorcha.

"Then give them to those who need them. We'll not return them to Lord Melville."

They did not leave without a farewell. Mounted on their horses and just pulling them around, they saw the hedge master come to the front door. He looked at them curiously, as if trying to recognize them, and then called in a voice soft as moss, "The Lord God carry you every road safe," and waved them away.

Oakes's face was grim as they turned their horses to Lord Melville's demesne. "You have a task and more ahead of you," he said to Anson.

"A task indeed, sir. But what was it that they were so fearful of report? That they would not take the sovereigns?"

Oakes shook his head. "Open your beclouded eyes, Fencible. What was on the table?"

"Herbs, some bowls."

"The other table."

"Books."

"And pens, and a tablet, and paper. I suppose you did not hear the pattering of feet above you either?"

"I did not."

"Drummer," said Oakes with a smile, "the hedge master was conducting school. That was why the girl stood by the staircase. They saw us, hustled the children to the loft, and did not have time to hide the books."

"And if they were to be reported . . ."

"Then the hedge master would be a fugitive and transported if caught. And that family would most certainly be evicted."

"And you will not report it."

"I will not, though it goes against the grain. I'll not favor the Lord Melvilles who grow fat and rich on others' land. But neither will I be saying that our good King George is wrong to forbid such schools, with their papist ways and teaching of the Irish tongue. It is English we should all be speaking, whether they massacre the saying of it or not."

"The hedge master was whipped for such teaching once before."

"And yet he does it again. He is either a brave man or a fool."

"A brave one for holding on to what belongs to him and his."

"A foolish one for holding on to it in a changing world."

"Well," said Anson, "a foolish man can be brave, and a brave man foolish."

"A good thought to hold while we dine on a brace of ducks with Lord Melville," replied Oakes.

Anson settled back into his saddle and let the rhythm of his mount sway him forward and back. He found his mouth watering at the thought of the ducks, but his stomach tightened at the image of sitting at Lord Melville's table again. If he was to sit at any table, he realized, he would rather sit at the long table in the cottage they had just left. He was surprised at the thought.

A sudden quick breeze as something hurtled past his eyes.

"Rogue!" screamed Oakes. Anson pivoted to see Oakes toppling from his horse and landing with his arm bent abruptly backward. His own horse gave a hurt whinny, and Anson turned back to see a wound bleeding across his mount's neck. He pushed down as hard as he could to keep the horse from rearing.

"Above. On the rise above!" yelled Oakes, holding his elbow.

But his horse was plunging forward with the pain, and Anson could hardly look away to see what was on the rise. A sudden leap, and Anson felt his feet leaving the stirrups and his body rolling down the neck of his horse, who jolted back at just that moment to somersault Anson into the air and land him on his back before galloping off in the direction of Dublin.

Anson lay stunned, finding that he had to will air into his lungs, and that it came with only the greatest effort. He wished the world would stop toppling quite so fast, and wondered why the sky had suddenly become so bright and at the same time so opaque. He also wished the voice nattering at him would go away and leave him to fall into sleep.

But it would not. "Drummer, get up. Get up. Up."

Anson rolled onto his side, surprised at how the steely pain could reach even into his very fingertips. He felt an arm pulling him upright.

"Are you hurt? Drummer, by God, answer. Are you hurt?"

Anson shook his head. "No, sir. Not as far as I can tell." Underneath the brightened sky he could just make out Oakes, standing with his sword in his left arm, his right hand tucked into his belt. He rolled to his knees, tried once, twice to stand, and finally staggered up, his knees bent against the world's spin.

"The young rogue from the cottage." Oakes grimaced. "He stood on top of the rise, just behind that wall, and lobbed stones down like bombs."

"Your elbow?"

"Damn the elbow. See to your mount, Drummer. And take care to . . ."

But Anson did not find out what he was to take care to do. Oakes's face turned suddenly white and he twisted to the ground, his sword clattering out before him.

# 5

*A*t New Barracks, Anson sat by the bed of Corporal Oakes, who was pulling his head back and forth to the rhythmic throb of his elbow. Through the night and all the next day it had swollen to three times its size and sprouted a bright network of red and black bulging veins. The least touch to his fingers sent a scream up his throat, and the fever that clutched him heated the room. Dr. Hoccleve had already bled him twice, and though the blood had spurted out strong from the glint of the knife, the fever had not abated.

The doctor stood at the foot of the bed, thoughtful and nervous, and started when Lieutenant Brockle walked in.

"Doctor, your report on Corporal Oakes."

The doctor hesitated. "I fear, sir, for the arm itself." He looked at Anson, hesitated again. "The fever does not abate. The elbow may well be splintered beyond repair, and should the arteries go the way they have begun . . ."

"What must you do?"

"I shall have to take the arm."

"Then you should prepare."

"It is not something I have done often. And it is not a procedure with sure success."

"Nonsense. Cannonballs will do it a score of times in any single battle."

"It is not the taking of the arm, sir. That is simple enough, if the patient is held down properly. It is the infection of the terrible wound that causes me to pause."

Lieutenant Brockle looked evenly at the doctor. "Surgeon, you have a duty to perform. If called upon to serve, can you?"

The doctor looked back at his patient. "I can, sir."

"Then prepare. And you, Drummer. You are to report to the colonel and Lieutenant Fielding. And for God's sake, Drummer, your leggings!"

Neither the colonel nor Lieutenant Fielding seemed inclined to notice Anson's leggings when he came to report, however. In the colonel's quarters, Anson stood at attention while the colonel strode back and forth. The shadows he threw were almost black in the lamplight, and they crossed Anson's face like slaps. His hands clasped and unclasped behind him, and he glared angrily at both Anson and the lieutenant.

"Rocks. I have two men taken down by a boy throwing rocks."

"Sir, one rock knocked Corporal Oakes's from his mount, while the other skittered the drummer's horse. It is hardly their fault that—"

"That what, Lieutenant Fielding? That our regiment is a corporal in arears? That a simple mission should fail so utterly? That that mission may become a rallying point for the disaffected around Dublin, and who knows how far beyond? Drummer, do you realize the disaster this represents?"

"Sir, it is hardly disaster."

"It is, Lieutenant. It is very much the disaster. The news will spread through every fen, every valley, every hedgerow: Two of His Majesty's Fencibles driven away, wounded, by a boy with rocks. It will be a point of pride for every Irishman, and soon we will all be ducking our heads outside New Barracks. Heaven only knows what lengths the giddiness of this news will inspire."

The colonel stopped pacing and stood behind his desk. He leaned down upon it heavily, then sighed deeply. "Lieutenant Fielding, organize the reprisal. The dawn after next."

"Sir, a boy throwing rocks hardly justifies a reprisal."

"If we do not deal with a boy throwing rocks, Lieutenant, we will be forced to deal with an entire county throwing firebrands. The dawn after next."

A sharp rap, then a messenger opened the door. "From Lieutenant Brockle, sir." The colonel read it, glanced at Anson, then sat down.

"See to it," he said, and the messenger saluted and left quietly. "Drummer, dismissed to your barracks."

"Sir, I had hoped to sit with Corporal Oakes."

"God's death!" roared the colonel, leaping up. "Do you not understand the simplest of orders? To your barracks, and confined there until the morning. Dismissed on the instant."

Anson retreated, white and shamed, and reached the barracks just as Sergeant Eyre had quieted the Fencibles for Lieutenant Brockle's messenger. "It's for poor Oakes, it is," he called. "Two lengths of stout rope, and four men as aren't afeared of blood. Blood, he says, like there's to be a flood of it. Blood everywhere, he says, and if it's like to make you drop, you shouldn't come."

"I'll be one of them for Oakes," came a voice.

"And I."

"And I. The day has yet to dawn when a bit of blood will turn me."

"And I'll come too," said Anson.

Sergeant Eyre shook his head. "No, this isn't a job for a drummer, especially one whose ribs have just been shivered. These three and myself, we'll manage. And we'll take care of his honor, who'll be up and ordering you about sooner than you'd wish." He smacked Anson on the shoulder. "Just you be ready to step out for him."

Anson watched them leave, then turned to his bunk, unbuckling the belts that swooped down from his shoulders. He stretched his coat against the foot of the bunk, then lay down, listening to the utter quiet that had crept into the air of the barracks. When one of the Fencibles began to whistle, he was shushed by two others. They heard the night fall around them. They could almost hear the stars jostle to their places.

And out of the darkest part of that night, out of its deepest, deepest blackness, they heard the shrill, strangled cry of a man beyond pain, beyond despair, beyond hell itself.

"So he's under the doctor's dirk then," said one.

A short scream, not as loud as the rest, and then all was quiet again.

A Fencible nodded toward Anson's bunk. "Oakes will be swaggering in here tomorrow dawn, as smart as you could ever hope to be."

"And smarter," another agreed. Then they both dropped into the kind of quiet that fills a room to smothering. Anson had to hold his mouth open wide just so he could breathe.

Oakes did not swagger in that next morning. When the Fencibles mustered to Anson's drums, they stood uneasy, casting looks toward the officers' quarters, where Oakes still lay. Anson yearned for leave to cross the quadrangle and rush up to Oakes, but he also half feared seeing him. What could he say to Oakes if he had lost an arm? It would mean the end of his career as a Fencible, retired as a corporal with a pension a beggar would spurn.

So Anson did not ask Sergeant Eyre for the leave, but he stood stony faced when the colonel emerged and walked across the cobblestones. He said nothing as the lieutenants at his side delivered the day's patrols and then dismissed them to mess. He turned back to his quarters without ever looking at Anson.

The rest of the day was desperately routine.

Anson found that he had not a spare moment. Lieutenant Fielding put him on patrol throughout the morning, and he had to finish the noon mess quickly so that he could repeat the patrol to Phoenix Park, where he was not allowed his usual hour of freedom. "Not on this day of the world, Drummer," said Lieutenant Fielding, without even a hint of a smile. By late afternoon Anson's feet had blisters in places they had never been before, yet he still stood while the Fencibles drilled their marching to his beat. Evening mess, and afterward a packing of his kit and an inspection of arms in preparation for a morning expedition. That night, Anson fell into his bunk and slept before he had turned once.

Lieutenant Brockle woke him in the dark. The Fencibles messed by candlelight and mustered to Anson's drum when the sky had just pinked. The air was heavy with a thick wet, and it was already warm—the first really warm day since Anson had come to New Barracks now so long ago. His uniform clutched at him as he stepped out behind the colonel. The sound of his drum fell dully behind him as the Fencibles marched through Dublin and headed toward the low, shaggy mountains that hunched to the south.

As the sun rose, the air—impossible though it seemed to Anson—grew wetter. He felt as though he were breathing underwater. The road squelched into reddened mud, and Anson found his boots growing heavier by the step. They crossed a small river where the water gurgled beneath a shroud of fog, and climbed a winding hill to a rocky defile, where he could stamp some of the mud off. At the bottom of the hill the fog hovered, waiting for them, and they passed into it so that it swirled around them and turned the landscape a yellowish gray. The unearthly quiet of that foggy world made all the Fencibles feel as if they walked half asleep. Whatever they passed—the odd cottage, a severe outcropping of rock, an ancient gallows—seemed to spring upon them suddenly, as if startled out of a dream.

Then the road began to rise again as the southern mountains gathered up the land, and they were out into the sunshine in air still wet but no longer yellow. Colonel Staplyton signaled with his hand, and Anson beat to a stop by the lightning-splintered towers of a keep, built to hold the country against an ancient wild enemy. Now yew trees had grown up in the courtyard and cattle grazed in what had been the great hall. Stones once hewn to their place lay scattered and cracked.

The Fencibles dispersed and sat on the ruined walls, tearing up elder bushes and hollies to make themselves room. Anson unslung his drum and leaned back against the big-leaved ivy that rioted all over the keep. To the east he could just see the darker blue of the sea, and if it had not been for the heavy green scent of the dark ivy, he could imagine smelling the saltiness of it.

He wished suddenly that Oakes were there beside him, pointing out the sea, looking to the southern rises. Nearby, cormorants stood on old, crazily angled headstones. They did not care about the bodies beneath them. Nor did they care that a regiment of Fencibles was on the march. Instead, they watched the sky. Anson wondered what Oakes would have said of them.

He took mess and then mustered the regiment to its files. On to Dundrum. There was, Anson remembered, to be a reprisal.

If the colonel had hoped for surprise, it soon was clear that there would be none. Rugged trenches had been gashed across the road wherever there was bogland to either side. Though the Fencibles could scramble down and up, the horses balked and had to be blindfolded and roughed across. But worse still were the two artillery pieces, of which Lieutenant Brockle had charge. At the first trench, he ordered the caissons around, where they immediately sank beyond their hubs into the muck. The team from the second caisson had to be unhitched and added to the team of the first before it could be pulled out, and then the trench filled in for the next caisson to cross, and even that stuck in the loosened earth.

By the time they had passed the fourth trench, Lieutenant Brockle was beyond words. If he could have sunk all Ireland with a curse, he would have uttered the abominable word and sunk gladly with it.

As Lieutenant Brockle grew more enraged, Colonel Staplyton grew more determined. When Anson watched him for a sign that they should stop to rest, or at least slacken the pace, he saw by the colonel's stone-jawed face that there would be no stopping on this day.

So Anson maintained his drumming, the rhythm to the beats ordering the steps of the Fencibles, though less and less so as even the low hills began to shadow the land.

And then they were at Dundrum.

Perched above them on a foothill, the village oversaw all roads from the south heading into Dublin. It was a place that travelers passed through, stopping for an hour at the single tavern and then moving on to Dublin. But even so, there was more than one traveler who looked at the quiet of this village and longed for it. The low steeple of its church pinned the village to the mountain, and the houses—all yellow with thatch, some of it green from the spring's new thatching—circled around it, held fast by its sacred weight.

Grazing sheep looked down from the meadows above, some of them already shorn, others as white as the hawthorn that was blossoming up in the reaches of the hills.

But none of the Fencibles was looking above the village. They all watched the group that had gathered by the foot of a stone bridge spanning a slough at the hill's foot—a group that was armed with high pikes.

The colonel wheeled about and motioned for Anson to halt. He looked at Anson a long moment. "Drummer, to the . . ." he began, then stopped. He shook his head, then turned to the Fencibles.

"Fix bayonets," and the Fencibles rang them to their muzzles.

"Lieutenant Brockle, you will establish your pieces there, and there. With dispatch, sir. Take what men you need."

Under the colonel's eye, it was indeed done with dispatch.

"Drummer, the advance," shouted the colonel, and taking his sword from its scabbard, he curved it toward the village of Dundrum.

Anson patterned out the advance and felt the body of the Fencibles move with him up and up toward Dundrum, toward the waiting pikes. The wound on his cheek began to throb.

So this was battle. This was what he had dreamed of for

so long: following his father against the enemy. Here were the ordered ranks, the bayonets and swords, the Fencibles marching as one. And soon they would thrust themselves like a wedge into the men waiting for them, thrust themselves in among the pikes, heedless of the blood and the screams, driving on and on until the enemy's back was broken and the Fencibles and the king had won the field.

Anson wondered if glory made other Fencibles feel sick.

But there was to be no battle on this day. A rolling boom from behind them signaled that Lieutenant Brockle had fired his first shot. Anson heard the ball high above his head, shrieking with its passing, but he did not see its landing.

The men with the pikes did. Some ran back into the village. Others wavered a moment, then banded together and shouted across the gulf at the Fencibles, shouting defiance and hate, waving their pikes with their bitterness. Then they too turned and ran back into the village. Only when the Fencibles reached the bridge did they find that the men had dropped its stones down into the slough, and that it was impassable.

The colonel would not waver.

Anson felt the eyes of Dundrum upon them as the Fencibles tore the rest of the bridge down, in an hour undoing a work that had stood six hundred years. The first stones sank quickly into the mire of the slough, but the next sank more slowly, then not at all, until a path reached across and the Fencibles marched into the deserted streets of Dundrum.

It was by now late dusk, and the sky was bright red and yellow with the promise of good weather the next day. The streets of Dundrum were dark, though, each of the house-fronts shuttered and covered with shadow. Not a single light showed. Not even a dog barked.

"Portfires," commanded the colonel.

Lieutenant Fielding rode beside the colonel. "Sir, to burn the town . . . How far such measures are politic, God alone knows."

The colonel looked at him evenly. "If God alone knows, Lieutenant, he has not spoken to me of it. Nor, I fancy, to you. Portfires. You will fire the town starting to the south and west, working back to this position."

"Sir," began Lieutenant Fielding.

"You will instruct the officers to be on guard against any looting, any excess of any kind."

"Yes, sir. Excess of any kind."

"Drummer, the advance." And so they marched on into the center of Dundrum, the portfires glowing eerily with their weird lights.

In the graying dusk, Anson could see the rags of families heading up into the hills to the south, many carrying great cloth-bound bundles between them. Some had children—and even old people—on their backs. They turned often to watch the advancing Fencibles and then stood still as they saw the thatch of their houses go up in orange bursts. House after house caught, the slow breezes whipped up by the heat, until soon the Fencibles no longer needed the portfires. It was as if the Devil himself were blowing the flames, and the town's light threw livid colors up and down the hills.

Anson felt the solid heat at his face. Smoldering ashes fell around him, and he wiped them from the head of his drum. The smell of scorching tightened his breath, but as he watched each of the houses erupt into flames, he felt a strange and uncanny exhilaration deep in his guts. This was for Oakes. This was for a man with a lost arm and a lost career. This was reprisal. He grinned wildly at the other Fencibles. Some ran up and down the main roads of Dundrum, shouting and dancing before the fire, holding their muskets above their heads, heedless of the shouts of their officers.

Anson found himself shouting, trying to eclipse the roar of the flames. He began to pound on his drum. When the high rafters of the church in the town square fell into themselves and sent a cavalcade of sparks high into the lit sky, he squealed with the delight of it, with the utter, laughable, splendid delight of it.

And then, suddenly, there was Lieutenant Fielding standing in front of him, grabbing the sticks from his hands. His face was grimed and sooty, and it seemed to Anson as if his eyes were wet. "This, sir," he said angrily, "is not the work of Fencibles."

Anson stared at him, caught in mid shout. "But sir, Oakes . . ."

"You know Oakes. Would he be of a mind that this be done for him?" He thrust the sticks back at Anson. "Sound the recall, though God alone knows if they will answer."

Anson began to tap out the pattern.

"Sound it, Drummer. For God's sake, sound it loud."

And as loudly as he could, Anson banged out the recall against the flames. And slowly, reluctantly, the pattern of obedience laid itself upon the Fencibles, and they came back from the fire, came back from the burning of Dundrum.

In ranks, they recrossed the slough. In ranks, they marched a quarter mile back toward Dublin. And in ranks, they coughed out the choking smoke that filled the air about them.

Before the road turned and hid the town, the colonel stopped his mount and looked back. Anson turned with him and cried out at what he saw. If the ground had exploded and hot lava had rained down for day after day after day, Dundrum could hardly have looked the worse—if there could be said to be a Dundrum anymore. In the gathered darkness the village glowed in red embers, except where a corner was blocked out for a moment by a billow of smoke. Occasionally, a house would collapse its rafters and bright flames would reach up, lighting up the undersides of the clouds that hovered above the ruins.

The colonel rode up behind Anson. "There, my boy, is the end of your mission. A message to all Ireland that no Fencible may be attacked with impunity. To attack a Fencible is to attack king, country, God himself. And so this."

"Yes, sir," answered Anson, and tasted bile in his mouth.

Four hours later, when they were barely outside Dublin, a messenger sent out from New Barracks pulled up his horse just short of the colonel.

"News?" the colonel asked.

"It's Oakes, sir."

The colonel nodded. "Dead, then?"

"Sir, the doctor was never able to stop the bleeding."

"Well," said the colonel, "he has already had his vengeance."

CHAPTER

6

*H*aving had his vengeance, Corporal Oakes seemed to disappear from the regiment. His mess and kit were quickly cleared out and sent back to his family in Staffordshire. And no one mentioned his name for the bad luck it would bring.

But Anson could not forget. Through the long trek back from Dundrum, through the next rain-driven days, through the early gray dawns that barely separated themselves from the nights, he could not forget. He heard Oakes's voice, thought of him in a thousand moments, and wondered what he would have said to the burning of a village in his name.

And Dublin did not forget either. The city breathed nervously, as if it were waiting for the next reprisal and wondering which side would begin it. Urgent messages came in from London, one from the king himself, urging the Fencibles to guard the new mansions going up across the river on Henrietta Street. Colonel Staplyton grumbled, then dispatched regular patrols to the fine houses. At Lord Melville's complaining, the colonel began to send patrols to guard his demesne as well.

If Colonel Staplyton muttered and complained about the stretching of his forces, Anson was just as glad of it. Each morning, he left New Barracks with the patrol that Lieutenant Fielding pulled out, crossed the River Liffey—never mind the stink of early-morning fish that clung to its oily surface—and marched onto the wet cobblestones of Capel Street. Above him, the masts of the ships that had drawn up by the Grattan Bridge tipped back and forth and dripped the fog from their rigging. The windows of the Boot and Shoe Warehouse hard by the river were shuttered tightly, but in the Burton Law Offices, the lamps of the early clerks were already lit.

On to Henrietta Street, where the first of the mansions that would line that road stood already framed and half bricked. Gray men with pack horses cleared away the rubble from the homes that had once held Irish families and now held the hundreds of rats that clambered up from the river each night. On Henrietta Street, the stink of the fish had faded, but the air was still, warm, and wet. Anson preferred the stink.

By the time the patrol marched back toward the Liffey, Capel Street had awakened. Long-gowned ladies strolled the flagstone walks, and carriages spurted along the street. From opened windows, maids beat carpets and apprentices looked out longingly. Men of business held the ruffles of their shirt fronts to their noses to blot out the smells; they waved gold-headed canes at the beggars who crouched to them. In the gutters, lean dogs nosed along to see what had washed down during the night. They scampered away from the workmen rolling barrels of sweet ale, the iron hoops clattering against the stones and sometimes throwing up a spark.

Wherever Anson looked, there was life and movement, but there was no talk, no chatter. At any sharp noise, the ladies scurried to the nearest shop and windows slammed shut overhead. And no one would look at the patrols. No one would notice them.

Except, one particularly wet morning, Sorcha O'Leary.

She stood under the windows of the Military State Lottery office, her boots only a little muddier than the hems of her long gown, her shawl tight across her shoulders, her bonnet as wet and dripping as if she had just pulled it from the river. As soon as she saw that Anson had spotted her, she stepped into the street, her hands outstretched, and dropped a folded note onto the top of Anson's drum. Then, without looking at him, she scurried away toward the Liffey.

Startled, Anson missed the trill as he grabbed the note and shoved it into his breast pocket. He felt his stomach screw to a tightness and his face redden at the rebuke from Sergeant Eyre.

"If you'll be going to the ladies, Drummer, you'll not be courting when on patrol."

"Yes, sir."

"It's hardly the boy's fault if the ladies cannot stay from him," suggested one of the Fencibles.

"You'll need to be looking to yourself, young Staplyton."

"It's not himself he's looking at, you sod."

"And to think that he's naught but a drummer and already taking notes and such. Like as not there will be love tokens wrapped inside."

"With a sweet curl of hair."

Anson began to pound louder to drown out the flurry of suggestions that accompanied his march with the patrol.

Back at New Barracks, he opened Sorcha's note on his bunk.

"Look at him, Sergeant. Have you ever seen a drummer so eager?"

Anson turned over.

"Is it to be tonight, young Staplyton?"

"Leave the boy alone now," gruffed Sergeant Eyre. "He won't be courting this day, not with the drills the colonel has ordered. Drills that will wear all your tired arses to a frazzle, I'll be bound."

Sergeant Eyre was right. To a frazzle. If the Fencibles were not on patrol, they drilled on St. Stephen's Green through the long day and into the long dusk. And with the

93

promise of a morning inspection, there were kits to be cleaned, uniforms to be straightened, and for Anson more errands than a single drummer could ever hope to run.

During all the cleaning and the drilling and the patrolling, Anson thought of one thing only: Sorcha's message. She would meet him in St. Michan's Church. She would wait for him until he came.

But it was only after evening mess of the next day that he found the free hour, and he was sure that she would not be there. Still, he walked quickly out of New Barracks after bolting down his mess, his sense of Fencible dignity barely keeping him from a run, wondering the whole time what it was that made him so eager to see her. Especially now that Oakes was dead.

He wondered if Oakes would have wanted him to see her, or whether he was betraying Oakes's memory.

As he crossed the river, he could see the medieval tower of the church beginning to redden in the gathering dusk, and his steps slowed. It was the first time since Dundrum that he had been alone in Dublin, away from New Barracks, away from any patrol. He suddenly missed the cheerful severity of Sergeant Eyre, especially when the faces that had turned away from him while he was on patrol now looked at him with curiosity and anger as he passed quickly along Capel Street. When he turned up the narrower streets toward St. Michan's, he felt the sudden dark quiet of the place thicken around him. He could not help looking over his shoulder, or watching the windows open above him, or starting when he was sure that he had heard a muttered "damn Fencible" from an alley that led nowhere but to darkness.

At the last, he half walked, half trotted into St. Michan's and stood breathing heavily in its cool dimness. Its stained windows filtered the light into cobalts and azures, coloring the sturdy pillars that thrust themselves up from the limestone vaults beneath. Anson had heard stories of those vaults and of the mummified dead whose mouths gaped weirdly. He shuddered with the chill that came at the thought of what lay just beneath his feet.

And then suddenly there was Sorcha, moving out of the dimness and standing in front of him, the stain of yesterday's wetting still showing on her bonnet and across her shawl. "You've come then," she said, and her eyes lowered.

Anson had thought a hundred times of what he should say at this moment. How he would accuse her. How he would tell her that her brother had killed his friend. How all of Dublin was in an uproar over what he had done. Good God, all of Ireland might well be in an uproar. But he said none of this.

"You'll pardon," he began, then stuttered to a halt. "You'll please to pardon my long . . ." and his voice withered to a quietness as he saw that she was crying.

"You'll not be naming him, my Roddy. Not my Roddy. He'll be hanged for sure, and then where will I be? Me and mine? If we're not transported ourselves, we're sure to be turned off the land. Sure to be."

Anson was stunned. He had not expected this. But at the thought of Oakes, he hardened. "If your brother had not . . ."

"He never meant to kill. Never. Though all the saints above know we've had the provocation to it. He threw stones is all. Just stones, hoping that he could come home and brag to all who would hear how he thumbed his nose at two Fencibles. He never thought that it would come to this. He never thought it would."

"But it has come to this," Anson said.

"Sure, it has."

In the dimness of St. Michan's, a long silence lay between them. The bells tolled their holy sounds softly at the passing of the hour, and the filtered lights climbed up the pillars and grew deeper. Anson felt himself about as far as he could possibly be from Staplyton Manor in Gadshall. If the world had turned itself upside down and he had found himself on its nether side, he could hardly have been farther from it.

"What is it you want me to do, then?" he asked.

She drew a long breath. "What I want you to be doing is to let him be. To not tell his name that threw the stones at you. Unless you've already told it."

"I have not."

96

"Then, sir"—and she reached out and took his hand—"then I beg you to hold it into yourself."

"A Fencible's loyalties are to his king, to his country, to his fellow Fencibles."

She released his hand. "I've no claim on you for your loyalties. But you hold so much over me, I do ask for you to understand. What is it you would be doing if you had seen your own father struck down?"

"By God, Sorcha, it was a terrible thing. And I'm as sorry as anyone can ever be to have been a part of it."

She stared at him, her head tilted to one side. "You truly are, then. You truly are. Our hedge master said he was sure that it was so, but I would not be believing it. Nor my Roddy."

"No man becomes a Fencible to do such things."

"And when such things are done, what must a Fencible be doing then?"

The question filled St. Michan's. What was a Fencible to do, when such things were done?

Anson turned from her. "My life is the life of a Fencible. It is my only life, and I have been living it since the moment I was born." He paused. "I try to understand about your brother. I do try. But you must know too that I am a Fencible."

"And is it the work of a Fencible to give over a boy to the noose?"

"It is the work of a Fencible to guard the king's realm."
Even as he spoke, Anson regretted the words. He sounded
like Lord Melville.

"Then, Fencible," said Sorcha, her voice carrying
sudden scorn, "you have found your own way to erase what
happened in the yard of my house. You betray your own self."

"It is hardly betrayal to hand over a murderer."

"A boy who throws stones is a murderer, is he? And you
who watched my da and brother shot down by a regiment
for a horse should not hold the word 'murderer' in your own
mouth."

Another long silence, and the light growing dimmer all
the while.

"You'd best be back to New Barracks, then, and do what
you must," Sorcha said at last. "Do what you must. Only this
one thing," and she grabbed his hand again with a desperate energy. "If you are who the hedge master thinks you are,
and who I hope you are, come out from Dublin and see the
hedge school. See what it is we must do to keep what has
been ours since before memory. Before you make my Roddy
a fugitive."

"If I'm to get leave, I . . ."

"Come and see," she insisted.

Anson weighed his worlds in his hands. It was not an
easy weighing.

Sorcha leaned forward to him and whispered, "And,
Anson Staplyton, stay to the lighted ways tonight. Keep out

of the alleys. That way your grave lies dug." She released his hand and let the shadows take her. Anson stood alone. Very alone.

When he came out of St. Michan's, it was mostly dark, the streets black except for the pools of yellow left behind by the lamplighter working his way along Church Street toward the river. Anson looked once down the empty streets that bent back and forth on their way to Capel, then turned to follow the lamplighter, stopping to watch him reach up, flit the glass to, and then ignite the wick.

"You'll be out late for a Fencible. And a young Fencible at that," he said, without looking at Anson.

"Later than I expected to be."

"There's those that would see opportunity there."

"Opportunity?"

"Those that once lived in Dundrum, or knew those that did."

"Then I had best be off to New Barracks."

"You had best."

But Anson lingered a moment, still watching the old lamplighter. "And are there really those that hate the king's Fencibles so very much?"

The lamplighter looked evenly at Anson. "Ask the men of Drogheda, if you can, those whose heads were set on pikes in my grandfather's day for being Catholic. Or ask the men of Wexford, who were strangled or drowned for the same. Or ask those families of Leinster or Munster, those that lost their lands or saw their nearest and dearest bound as servants to the Indies. Or ask those that fled their green homes into exile. Yes indeed, boyo, there are those that hate the king's Fencibles that much."

Anson stepped back as though from a blow as the lamplighter resumed his work. He wondered if the streets had ever been so black, ever been so very quiet. At the quay, he headed to Capel Street, walking stiffly but quickly, passing groups that quieted at his approach and whose murmurs scoured his back. At the bridge, he turned at footsteps but saw nothing. Passing St. Stephen's Green, he heard more footsteps but still could see nothing.

Then, a stifled cry and a shout from the green, and Anson rushed to a sprint, pushing through the streets of the city, missing one turn, circling back in the dark, missing it again, all the time breathing and panting for fear of what he could not see. Then, by chance, the right street and the way to New Barracks, whose lamps glowed brightly against the early fog that was thickening the night. Anson ran with his hands out in front of him, ran without thought, ran for fear that even now, in the last moments before safety, he would feel a hand upon him, or the thudding impact of a cartridge between his shoulder blades.

Sergeant Eyre had perhaps never before seen a Fencible so eager to embrace him as young Staplyton that night.

In fact, all of New Barracks seemed to have hunkered down that night, watching through the fog, listening for footsteps, holding muskets primed and at the ready, checking the priming against the damp of the night air. As Anson lay in his bunk, thinking of the run to New Barracks, of St. Michan's, of Sorcha, Lieutenant Fielding was striding deliberately from gate to gate, gathering his reports, cheering where cheer was needed, guffawing louder as the fog grew thicker. His voice carried even to the bunks, where Anson heard it and smiled.

A longing for home filled him. A longing to see his sisters, his mother, his own room. To draw into himself the smells of his own kitchen, the familiar tastes of his mother's puddings. He thought of the high grass that thickened over the hills past Staplyton Manor, and of how the wind blew across it and bowed the seed heads to a bob, carrying the green scent and lacing it with sweet clover and thyme and mint, so you could hardly know if you were breathing or tasting the air.

"Come and see," Sorcha had said.

Anson decided he would. And he would get leave that very night.

But when he knocked and entered the colonel's quarters, still feeling the wet hands of the fog on his shoulders, he quailed. Lieutenant Fielding and Lieutenant Brockle stood on opposite sides of the colonel's desk, the colonel seated between them, and the heaviness in the air told Anson that he should be back in the barracks. The colonel held up his hand at Anson's "Sir." Anson would wait.

"Colonel," Lieutenant Brockle challenged, leaning far over the desk, "harsher measures are called for, not only in Dundrum, but out to the west as well."

"Harsher than the burning of a village?" asked Lieutenant Fielding.

"Yes, if need be. Harsher still. Or there will be many another village in flames before rebellion is stamped out."

"There is no rebellion. You bring up phantoms, Lieutenant," said the colonel slowly.

"By God, if only there were one and we could act instead of holding here in New Barracks."

"We have acted," said Lieutenant Fielding.

"And still, whoever it was threw the stones remains free, and Oakes is six feet under. Do you think the villain is not up every dale, in every farmyard, encouraging others to follow his path, a path trodden with such complete impunity till now?"

"I think not, Lieutenant Brockle," said Lieutenant Fielding earnestly. "By Oakes's own account, the stones were thrown by a boy. Just a boy, sir. There is no conspiracy here."

"Of such boys, men are made. Of such men, rebellions."

"Colonel," said Lieutenant Fielding, "more reprisals will push the people toward rebellion. Even here in Dublin, where we can be assured of loyalty, there is a kind of surly anger at our presence now. I beg you, sir, let the incident be."

"And I say, sir, a firm hand is needed. A firm hand." Lieutenant Brockle folded his arms across his chest. "The insolence of these Irish is beyond imagining. Certainly beyond the imagining of any gentleman. Surely this last outrage at Lord Melville's demesne is proof enough."

"Outrage?" asked Lieutenant Fielding.

"You should read the reports, Lieutenant. The stone cross that Lord Melville placed in the center of his rose garden was stolen two nights ago and has now disappeared. The roses were torn out by their roots, the garden mangled beyond repair."

"The loss of a few roses is hardly cause to panic, Lieutenant Brockle."

"But it is cause for action, sir. Colonel, we cannot allow any insolence against the king to stand unrequited. We cannot."

The colonel stood slowly. "The responsibility is, of course, mine, Lieutenant Brockle." He sighed deeply. "There will be no need for another Dundrum. That would be beyond reprisal and become provocation. But there is a need for a continued firm hand, as you put it—the firmness a father would use toward his children."

"Sir, these are not children we govern," said Lieutenant Fielding. "They too are of a proud and ancient culture, as ancient as any that England itself can boast. And like us, they will not bear injury well, nor forget even the smallest of slights."

Lieutenant Brockle clucked his tongue. "Some tribal wars, a few hermits perched out on crags like birds—hardly a culture at all. And whatever culture might be claimed is, after all, forbidden by the king's law."

"Thank you, gentlemen. You have been more than helpful. We will restrict ourselves to stronger, more frequent patrols. They are not to provoke, but neither are they to brook insult. Lieutenant Brockle, you will draw up an edict forbidding the green flags that I have had occasion to see, and draw a patrol—of sufficient strength, mind you—to make a foray past Lord Melville's demesne."

"And to the matter of the boy who threw the fatal stones, sir?" asked Lieutenant Brockle.

The colonel turned to Anson. "Yes, the boy who threw the fatal stones." He looked at Anson. "What have you to say to that, Drummer?"

Anson started as the two lieutenants turned to him. He could almost see Sorcha standing beside them, the dark of St. Michan's around her. "Sir, I'm sure he should be punished if caught. Though I daresay that he had no notion that he might be about a killing."

"Intentions count but little in this world, young Staplyton. What matters is the act," returned Lieutenant Brockle.

"Then is this world a doomed place," said Lieutenant Fielding quietly, "when even the best of intentions count for nothing."

"Again, thank you, gentlemen. Dismissed." With grave and formal bows, both lieutenants took their leave.

"So you would try to understand this perpetrator?" asked the colonel.

"Sir?"

"He had no notion that he might be about a killing?"

"I believe not, sir."

"One would think that you knew the scoundrel. Silence from you. Well, I will not ask what you might not in honor answer . . . if your silence is indeed honorable."

"Sir, I have come about another matter entirely, though perhaps not so unrelated. I would ask leave for tomorrow."

The colonel looked evenly at Anson. "To what end, sir? More silence. More honorable silence." The colonel sat down, placed the tips of his fingers end to end, and considered. Anson had a sudden desire to reach out and stroke those hands, hands that he had not felt for many a year.

"Anson, you do understand what being a Fencible entails."

"I do, sir."

"And where your loyalty lies."

"Yes, sir."

"And you do understand, Anson, that what you do reflects on your commanding officer—all the more because I am your father."

"I do understand that, sir."

"Yet I fail to understand your silence."

"I am not sure I understand it myself, sir. I ask this leave to see if I might come to understand."

"You will go alone?"

"If you will permit, sir."

The colonel stood, his fingers drumming a pattern on his desk. "It has not been so long," he said softly, "since I stood where you stand now. I was so eager then to stand where I stand now." He shook his head. "You have leave until evening mess, Drummer. Report to Lieutenant Fielding upon your return."

"Yes, sir."

"And for God's sake, let us have no further incident. I will not have more than one Dundrum to think about in my declining years."

"No, sir."

The colonel strode up and down his quarters. To Anson, he seemed to be arguing within himself, but nothing in his tone suggested this. "Dismissed, Drummer. And ask Lieutenant Brockle if he would do me the courtesy of seeing me again tonight."

"Good night, sir," and Anson bowed out the door.

"Come and see," Sorcha had invited him. Tomorrow he would come and see.

# CHAPTER

## 7

*A*nson found Sorcha alone the next morning, peering out the window of her farmhouse. "Perhaps," she said, greeting him in the yard, "you'd do better to be wearing this. A red coat will not be the most welcome in the places we'll be to." She held out a brown jacket, and with only a moment of hesitation, Anson put it on.

Perhaps Sorcha meant to show him the beauty of the world, or perhaps she meant only to delight herself. But in either case, she led Anson past the farmyard and up an ascent that rose so quickly that soon they were hand in hand, helping each other clamber over the mossy boulders that jutted out unexpectedly. All around them the ferns and lichens softened the rocks. When Sorcha turned him so that he would look out from the hill, he hardly knew whether he was short of breath from the climb or the sight.

"The yellow is gorse," she said, "and the white, hawthorn. The purple—see how it bows to the wind—that purple is heather, and just beyond is laburnum—all the gold there. Past them, where the water is bright green—those are the peat marshes we cut our turf from. When the tide is out, the water is as brown as a seal."

She led him higher up the hillside, until they were walking on a path that cut its way through thick briars covered with sharp green prickles. "You'll not want to be falling into these," she said, and Anson was startled to find how much her laughter delighted him. He followed just behind her, sweating in the heat of the day but holding his jacket close to keep the brambles from snatching at it.

She reached the top before him, and when he stood by her side and looked down, he did not have to speak to tell her what she herself knew. If this had not been Eden itself, then the Lord God had erred. The slopes of six hills, greener than green, their sides silvered by streams, lolled down toward a reedy lake. Some of the water rushed white and tumbling into the lake, gushing out of a fault in the limestone rock; some fell gently from one small pool to another before sliding through the reeds. Still more dashed down in a great brawl to the bottom, sending up a mist that rose to a rainbow. And in the lake, closer to the stiller pools, swans, maybe a score or more, glided through the water, while brown herons picked their thin-kneed way, poking long bills into the mud.

Here the slope was easy, and they ran down it, tensing

the backs of their legs to keep from rolling over, laughing with the ease and pleasure of it, all the while heading for an old stone tower set on a shelf of rock jutting to the edge of the lake. It had seemed small from the heights, but the closer he got, the more Anson was surprised at its rocky strength and stern brooding. The red granite stones of its curves were undressed, and dark-green ivy had climbed across its roughness and torn at its mortar. The south side had collapsed, and out of it grew a dark yew tree, its branches thrusting through the collapsed wall and even out one of the narrow windows. Heavy with mist, the branches waved like sodden feathers.

On the far side of the tower and hard against it leaned a small chapel, its stones lying loosely one on top of the other. A square stone cross stood out front like a guardian, a sternly delicate carving of hard granite but traced through with fine lacery. Water dripped from the circles of its patterning. In fact, the lake water wet the ground almost to the chapel doorway, where moss had grown so thickly that Anson could have reached in with his hand up to his wrist before he met stone.

"It's to here that I've brought you then," said Sorcha, speaking loudly against the rushing of the water.

Anson, panting for his breath, looked around him, feeling as though he were suddenly in some tale of enchantment where time meant nothing. He might be out of the world, for all he knew, in a place where anything could happen and he would hardly be surprised. It was a place that would have brought Oakes to a wonder.

With the memory of Oakes, Anson felt himself harden, and he released Sorcha's hand. "It's a beauty of a place, no denying," he said. "But there's other places in the king's realm that would match it."

"There speaks a Fencible," came a voice from out the chapel, and Anson turned to see the hedge master leaning against the doorway, his arms crossed lightly in front of him. "Sure, there are other places in the king's realm as beautiful, but they are hardly beautiful because they are the king's. They are beautiful because they carry the soul of their people."

"Or," replied Anson, "the soul of the people is beautiful because it carries in it the land."

The hedge master raised an eyebrow and uncrossed his arms. "Well said, young Fencible. And it might be true, after all. And even if not, it gives me hope to hear an Englishman believe it."

"We are all Englishmen now, sir."

"We are all the king's subjects, indeed. But we are not all Englishmen, young Fencible. If this is a truth that has escaped you, you might learn it from Lord Melville. He is most eager to teach it."

"All Englishmen are not Lord Melville."

"They are not. And that, sure, is what gives this old

heart hope. Come into the tower now, Fencible, and see what it is you are here to defend against."

Anson walked behind the hedge master, Sorcha following. Inside, broad blocks of sunlight came in through the ruined south wall, as well as through four narrow windows, one still with a shard of the blue glass that had once spanned it. And in that sunlight, in chairs pushed out from the dark shadow, twelve boys sat in nervous silence, some reading, some writing, but all glancing furtively over their shoulders at the Fencible who had come among them.

"The Dear Lord knows it is hardly a proper school. But St. Gobnet herself led us to it."

"St. Gobnet?"

"St. Gobnet, saint of those in hiding. Long ago, on a day when Ireland was almost at its end, she called the bees from their hives to blind the army that would destroy her." He pointed to one of his students. "The young one there," said the hedge master, "he's been at the mastering of Horace and is now on to Livy. The one there is finished with his lines of Augustine. There isn't a one who cannot be at the reading of Virgil in the Latin, and some Homer in the Greek. They would all be to Cicero now, had you Fencibles left us our libraries. But"—and he turned back to his students, smiling broadly—"sure it is that they would rather be hearing of the sweet ringing of St. Ciaran's bell, or of Patrick himself, or of Brendan and his sailing. And each boyo can tell the stories of his people in his own tongue, of the glories of High King

Brian Boru, or of the follies of Dermot MacMurrough. It hardly seems enough to bloody the bayonet of a Fencible."

Anson stared at the quiet rows in front of him. For this, the hedge master had been lashed at his drumming. For this, the hedge master risked being transported.

"Still," said Anson, turning to look at him, "what you do is against the king's law."

"It is," agreed the hedge master.

"And you risk so much for so little."

"I would risk more for less. Young Fencible, in my grandfather's time—and not so long ago that was—a man could wander over all these hills and find farms where he would be welcome. Inside, kitchen fires would blaze against joints of beef and mutton, hissing in the twirling jacks. Beside them would be a cauldron of tubers, boiling in sweet herbs and waiting for the ewe's butter to flavor them. A plank table would stand set for him, with a fowl plucked and boiled for the joy of the day. And milk and butter, cheese and cold ham, and afterward ale and the story—always the story told in the old way, in the old tongue.

"Now all is gone, long ago gone. What we grow is loaded onto ships for well-fed mouths in London, and little enough is left for the hungry mouths of Ireland. When the English want even our farms for their sheep, they put off five score of farmers and turn the fields to grassland. For the farmers, there's naught but the Dublin poorhouse, where they sit the livelong day and mallet stones into gravel to receive an English penny."

"Teaching Horace and Livy will do nothing for that," Anson pointed out.

"No," agreed the hedge master, "it will not. But it is more than our food that England takes. We cannot speak with the tongue of our fathers. Even our names are forbidden: To the Fencibles I am only Sullivan, not the O'Sullivan my mother named me. But we will not forget who we are, though our teachers and poets are hunted down. We will not have a generation grow up that does not know its own past."

By the time the hedge master had finished, he was breathing heavily and speaking more and more quickly. His students were no longer pretending to read. They were all watching, all listening to each word. It was as if Anson were no longer there. In fact, he felt he should not be there. When one of the students stood and spoke to the hedge master in lilting music that Anson could not understand, he felt again the otherworldliness of this place. It was as if he were hearing the sounds of the very land, but they were not for him.

The hedge master turned to Anson. "He asks if you would hear of Tara."

A long moment passed, as Anson wondered if even to listen to such a story would be a betrayal of the Fencibles.

But in this place, with the rushing of the water in his ears . . . "I would," he said.

The student steadied himself, cleared his throat, and began in a high, singsong voice, using the old tongue of the land and pausing now and again to let the hedge master translate for him.

"He speaks," said the hedge master, "of the seven ramparts of Tara that rose from the hand of Cormac, the son of Airt, the son of Conn of the Hundred Battles. They climbed one upon the other, higher and higher toward the sun over the Plain of Breg. On the seventh rampart that Cormac MacAirt built, there stood the Hall of the Throne, where the great treasures of Ireland hung: the spear of Lugh, against which none could maintain battle; the sword of Nuadha, whose wound was death; the cauldron of Dagda, that left none unsatisfied; and the Lia Fail, the stone that screamed at the crowning of every king of Ireland.

"It was from the ramparts of Tara that Midir the Proud carried Queen Etain to the blissful land where eyes flash with many lights and where the pasture is ever green. It was from Tara that King Diarmuid sent out the word that brought all the tribes of Ireland into allegiance to the one high king. And it was from Tara that King Laoghaire first looked out and saw the torch of St. Patrick himself, bringing a new light to Ireland.

"But on another night, the last king of Tara woke to a terrible dream. He dreamed that he saw a mighty tree whose branches scraped the clouds of heaven, and whose roots were the foundations of the earth. And around that trunk were small men, each with his own small axe. And each and every one of them chipped at the tree. And though at first they made hardly a mark, the time came when they were through the bark, and then into the heartwood, and the mighty tree came shrieking down with a crash that tore the stars out of the skies. And when the last king woke, there were tears in his eyes.

"And so today the seven ramparts are gone. The mighty hall, all gone. And there is nothing to mark the place of Tara but the high grass that bows to the wind."

The boy sat down. All was very quiet, very still. Even the sounds of falling water seemed to have paused at the ruin of Tara, and Anson felt himself in the presence of something terribly old, older than he could imagine. When he turned at Sorcha's touch, he was not surprised to see the tears that welled in her eyes. What he was surprised at was that he had to blink back his own.

But then the world came back. A clattering and breathless red-faced boy hardly half Anson's size dithered into the chapel, his wind so gone that he could only bend and point. The hedge master leaned down to him and held him up by the shoulders, trying to make out his hoarse whisper. Then he stood.

"Two English soldiers, three perhaps, up over the crest and just out of sight." He looked at Anson. "We always leave one boy to watch," he said. "We ask those with the sharpest eyes." He tousled the boy's black curls. "Sure, St. Gobnet is busy enough these days that she might be overlooking the likes of us."

Within moments, the boys had gathered up books into a basket and had scattered from the chapel, each clambering up a different hill, some fording the streams and heading off to the far side of the lake. "You'll be remembering what it is you've seen here," said the hedge master to Anson. Then he too was gone, clambering as quickly as any of the boys and cutting to a pass whose high grass and thick furze hid him as though the land itself had hunched over to protect its hedge master.

Sorcha picked up the basket of books, laid a square of bright cloth over it, and took Anson by the hand. "It may be nothing at all. It may be just a trick of the eye. But we'll not be leaving much to chance."

Together they climbed back up the hillside, Sorcha quiet, Anson wondering how it was that soldiers should have come to just this spot. They were silent together all the way to the farmyard, where Anson's horse stood tied side by side with Sorcha's goats.

"And how is it to be with my Roddy?" Sorcha asked as he mounted.

Anson looked down at her from the height of his horse and felt certain, right then, that he would never bring harm to her or hers. He could not imagine such a thing. And yet the familiar itch of his red coat, donned again, the familiar ringing of the bit, and the firm feel of the stirrups—all these reminded him that he was a Fencible, and from a line of Fencibles. If a land could frame the soul of its people, his too had been framed. He could not help but be what he was. And he could not help but be proud of what he was.

But when he looked at Sorcha, and when he remembered the shots that had rung against the stone walls of the farmhouse . . .

"Sorcha," he said miserably, and then stopped. She was no longer looking at him. Anson turned to follow her eyes and saw, well off in the distance, three mounted soldiers riding briskly away, their red uniforms bright against the green furze.

"Do what you must do," she cried fearfully. She rushed back to the farmhouse, then turned at the doorway. "The Lord God carry you every road safe," she called, and was gone.

Suddenly Anson was not sure that there was any road safe.

He rode back to Dublin half expecting stones to come ricocheting down. He had not seen Roddy O'Leary at the cottage, nor had he promised to keep his name safe. But he knew he would, even though Roddy might be above him now, palming a rounded rock. Anson's eyes searched the heights, the hedgerows, the ditches that lined the road. His mount skittered, and he felt her sides twitching with the nervousness in him. He urged her to a brisk walk, then a trot, and resisted what he yearned to do: Give her her head and get back to New Barracks. No Fencible would gallop like a frightened hare.

But even as his eyes darted back and forth, Anson knew that what twisted his stomach was not fear of stones, or at least not wholly fear. He was a Fencible, but what answer would he have given Sorcha had she not seen the other soldiers? And would the answer he might have given be one that would bring honor to a Fencible?

And where did a Fencible's honor—no, where did Anson Staplyton's honor—lie?

He had imagined a Fencible's life so clearly. His choices would be easy, because there would be only one choice: to follow the line of command. What he did would always be pure and honorable, because what he did, he did in the king's name. His life could never be otherwise.

And so later, when Anson saw the great billows of black, black smoke careening up, grasping and tearing at the clouds, he was almost glad of it. Here was duty with no choice; there was only one thing a Fencible might do at such a sight. He spurred his horse to it, galloping so fast that he could think of nothing but galloping, his mouth open to take in the heady wind, his eyes half-closed against the air's rebuff.

So he rode into Lord Melville's demesne.

Most of it was already afire. White heat had already

wilted the rows of fuchsia hedges and bowed the blooming rhododendrons to the ground. In the still-bright sunlight, the flames showed themselves as hysterical waves of rippled air, and the roar, the terrible hellish roar of the fire, made Anson's horse shy away. The great beams of the manor house fell like explosions, and as Anson watched, the cut-stone walls wavered, then wavered again and fell in a cataclysm, sending the smoke skyward in a frenzy, as though desperate to spread its pallor.

Over the roar of the flames came a terrified scream, and then another and another, and from around the far end of the house bolted Lord Melville's stable of horses, their tails jerked high into the air, ears back, eyes open and full. And behind them in a barking chorus came his hounds, who saw Anson and circled around him, then stood barking and baying at the ruined house, the hair behind their heads stiff and straight, their breaths coming in great confused gulps. Someone, at least, had opened the stables and kennels.

Anson wheeled his mare to a distance, then dismounted, sure that he could never urge her closer to the fire. Holding the collar of his coat in front of his face and one arm crooked over his head, he sprinted around the manor house, hoping he would find someone to tell him what had happened here—hoping that there was someone still alive in the inferno to do the telling.

At the back of the house, small fires had ignited in the gardens, scorching the flowerbeds and blackening the pruned fruit trees. Even the apple trees, far enough away to be safe from sparks, had dropped their blossoms in the heat, laying a pink carpet over the ground. It was there that Anson found the huddle of Lord Melville's servants, stooped and confused.

"All safe?" Anson cried.

The servants did not answer but moved respectfully apart to reveal the prostrate form of Lord Melville himself, his satin waistcoat unbuttoned and a rip along the side of his lavender pantaloons, now stained with smoke and grass. One servant held his head up, and another pressed a wet cloth to his forehead.

"Safe?" Lord Melville sputtered. "Safe? When madmen with torches run free about the countryside and not a single Fencible—not a single one, mind you—has patrolled the area within the last three days?" Lord Melville's voice rose half an octave. "It is inexcusable! Inexcusable! Three days of perfect freedom to those who would strike at the king's ministers." Lord Melville perched himself on his elbows. "Not to be borne. What is Colonel Staplyton about, that he should allow such uninhibited freedom to outlaws and traitors?"

Anson turned back to the manor house. The last wall was now tottering, waving back and forth as though a strong wind were battering at it. Then it dipped in, tried to lean back, dipped farther, and fell in a cataclysm of stone and fire and sparks. The huge roar of it surrounded them like monstrous pain, but then subsided. One last billowing, and the smoke grew less and did not rise quite so high. It was a small Dundrum, and Anson knew that the charred embers would glow red well into the night.

"Damn your impudence, man, of course I shall stand." Lord Melville jerked his arm away from the servant who pleaded with him to lie still. "Do you think an Englishman falters at such a moment? He does not. He does not. And I shall stand at the gallows when the Irish rogues who did such a thing drop. I shall stand with a hen wing in one hand and a glass of sherry in the other, and sip it as their throats rattle. But . . . my house."

As Lord Melville stood looking at the ruin, Anson thought that the man too might totter like one of the walls. He held his fists up in the air on both sides, as if clutching the throats of Irishmen. But his face slouched and, in the embers' red light, seemed in danger of melting. He took a single step forward, then dropped one hand. "It was Italian marble," he said weakly.

"Sir"—Anson bowed—"we should be away to Dublin."

"I would have had twice the trout stocked by next spring," Lord Melville answered, and stared blankly at the disaster. He dropped his other fist.

"Sir, we must be away to Dublin."

Lord Melville said nothing. He stood, swaying just a little. His servants looked at one another fearfully.

"Sir," said Anson again, touching him on the shoulder.

Lord Melville started. He drew his hand across his face, then seemed to puff himself up. "By God, Fencible, there will be hell to pay for this. By God, there will be. If these peat cutters thought life was hard before, they'll be on their knees begging that it may be so again before they have heard the end of this day's work." He glared around him, as if there might be some soul lingering nearby with a torch that he could grasp.

"Go gather the horses," he cried. "And you with him"—he shoved his servants toward Anson. "Then see if my coach is still intact. Fencible, you will escort me to New Barracks, where I shall lodge until I leave for London." He looked at the disaster of his house. "Hell to pay!" he cried out.

As he searched for the horses, Anson could hardly feel sorrow for Lord Melville, but he did feel sorrow for the ruin of the demesne. He thought of the perfect sets of books, their leather spines gold imprinted, and how they must have burst into flames one after another. He thought of the jasperware and the porcelain, of how each piece would have been shattered with the heat, if not smashed by a falling beam. He thought of the labor that had hewn one stone after another into place, of the symmetrical beauty of the place, and of the elegant planting that had made this world into a painting. Now it was gone, all gone.

Like Tara.

A servant found the horses grazing contentedly upwind from the house. Another found the coach, unharmed inside the stone carriage house, though even there the heat had been so great that the paint had run on the Melville coat of arms. Lord Melville paced impatiently as the harness was improvised, then clambered in without a backward glance at the house.

Having retrieved his own mount, Anson rode behind the coach. He paused for a moment at the ancient stone that had decorated the doorway, toppled and rolled away from the heated wreck. Its inscribed words were still clear and showed themselves up into the smoky air.

1524

REMEMBER VANITI OF VANITI
AL IS BY VANITI

Then he hastened after the coach as Lord Melville called out, wondering why the Fencible would delay so.

They were in New Barracks by nightfall, Anson reporting to Lieutenant Fielding, Lord Melville insisting upon an interview with Colonel Staplyton on the instant.

"What have you been about, young Staplyton?" asked Sergeant Eyre, back by Anson's bunk.

Anson wiped at the soot that coated his face. "Lord Melville's demesne was burned, sir. I've just now ridden in with him."

"Burned, has it?" Sergeant Eyre nodded. "And so we're for it, now."

# 8

$\mathcal{D}$ublin settled down to a quiet fortnight—quiet, perhaps, only because of the stepped-up patrols that Colonel Staplyton mounted. One young boy was caught chalking "Remember Dundrum" on the wall outside the quadrangle, and though Lieutenant Brockle urged that he be whipped as an example to all the wretched urchins of Ireland, Colonel Staplyton instead had him sent home under threat of transportation for his family, should he be caught again. If there was murmuring, it was behind closed doors, and not a single green flag showed to defy the king.

Inside New Barracks, Lord Melville prowled about as though he were himself in charge of the state of the Fencibles, and it was a state, he was sorry to say, that displeased him enormously. Enormously, sir. He found fault with their barracks, their uniforms, their kits, their rifles— even the sheen of their boots. Sabers were not sharp enough, wigs not powdered enough, marching not precise enough. And the drummer! Good Lord, the drummer was disgraceful! Mark the spots on his leggings.

"He'll be gone in ten days," whispered Lieutenant Fielding to Anson. But each day seemed ten, as Lord Melville patrolled the quadrangle, arms clasped sternly behind his back, pointing out the missteps and throwing contempt at Anson.

"How could there not be missteps with such drumming?" charged Lord Melville. The colonel merely nodded. "Have the men carry on, Lieutenant," he said, and left Lord Melville's cry hanging in the air.

"He'll be gone in five days," whispered Lieutenant Fielding. Anson calculated the hours.

And there were plenty of hours to count, for he was no longer part of the round of patrols. Each day as Lieutenant Brockle called them off, Anson's name was not listed. Instead, he was assigned to drill, and drill, and drill, all the while under Lord Melville's peering eye. When he asked Lieutenant Brockle about his new orders, Lieutenant Brockle looked at him sharply.

"Are you questioning your orders, Drummer?"

"No, sir."

"Are you unhappy with your orders?"

"No, sir."

"Then, Drummer, for the life of me I cannot imagine what you are about. Dismissed."

"Never you mind, boy," said Sergeant Eyre later that

night. "You'll be back on patrol once the times settle down."

But Anson was not quite sure that it was the times that were keeping him from patrol.

The days before Lord Melville's departure brought in the heat of early summer, breaking the Fencibles into a sweat at the march and drooping still-fresh green leaves, just a bit. During drill, Anson thought about the hills past Sorcha's farm and the wet of the ground and the cool breezes that wrapped like scarves around the hilltops. But here in New Barracks, the paving stones took in the sun, dried, and then baked, so that they gave out as much heat as they took in, and more.

On the evening before his departure, Lord Melville held a great banquet in the colonel's quarters. Anson was not invited. Instead, he sat outside the barracks, watching the moon rise and wondering how it would look from the top of those hills, and what Sorcha might say to him as they stood there hand in hand. There was a pleasure in sitting alone in the moonlight, a pleasure so tangible that he begrudged even Sergeant's Eyre's smile as he walked past, his hands behind his back and his face to the sky.

"Don't think too hard on her, young Staplyton," said the sergeant.

"Sir?"

Sergeant Eyre turned and grinned. "It wasn't so very long ago that I was a young boy sitting in the moonlight."

"No, Colonel," echoed Lord Melville's voice across the

quadrangle, "transportation is too good for the likes of him. And as for the other, hanging too good. You see what the lack of a firm hand has led to." Lord Melville's voice was slightly lispy.

"His ship leaves tomorrow," whispered Sergeant Eyre. "Pray God for good weather." With a wave, he strolled on.

Anson leaned back against the wall, his hands behind his head. It was fitting that the day had cooled to this beauty, that the moon was so perfectly round and clear, and that the stronger stars were still shining through its light. The whole world was celebrating Lord Melville's leaving.

"See if those broadsides do not bring in word." Lord Melville's voice again. "Why, Colonel, promised gold is more than enough to tempt even the most fanatically loyal. I'll be expecting word from you within the month. Within the month, I say again."

The familiar sound of the guard on duty came, passing back and forth across the quadrangle, his steps steady and sure, so automatic that Anson hardly heard them. From outside New Barracks, the heavy *clop, clop, clop* of a team of Clydesdales sounded, perhaps a last delivery to some brewery this night. A servant hustled across the quadrangle, two bottles in each hand and another tucked under the right elbow. A cheer came up from the colonel's quarters at his entrance, and then loud calls for toasts.

Anson went back inside.

The next morning, Anson marched out of New

Barracks for the first time since he had returned from Sorcha and the hedge master. Drumming carefully and precisely, he led the parade of Fencibles down to the River Liffey, then along its north side to the docks on the bay, where a double line of infantry stood at attention. Lord Melville rode in an open coach, disdainful of any attention that Dublin would give him. He would not even acknowledge the volley of muskets that saluted him as he passed St. Stephen's Green. He held a handkerchief to his nose at the fishy smells of the river, and at the scents of tar, sea slime, and indistinguishable scum that floated in the harbor.

The colonel himself paraded at the head of the Fencibles. When the procession came to a halt where the *Bonaventure* bobbed, he rode back to open the carriage door and escort Lord Melville to the ship. Lord Melville paused before he descended. "Colonel Staplyton, I remind you. If you wish to enjoy my patronage again, you will be sending me the news I wish to hear within the month. The month, I say." The colonel nodded, but Lord Melville, without waiting for an answer, strode across the dock and labored up the gangway, waving aside the eager hands that waited to help him aboard.

Perhaps it was only Anson's imagining, but it seemed to him that a great sigh went up from the Staffordshire Fencibles that day, that the wind suddenly freshened, and that the marching back was smarter than any they had ever performed.

The colonel, riding beside Anson, paused as the Fencibles wheeled in formation to take the Grattan Bridge. "An absolute marvel," he said. "The most proficient drumming these ears have heard in their long career of listening to drummers." If Anson had not known better, he might have said that the colonel was actually beaming. Perhaps he too was glad that Lord Melville was on his way to England.

Anson wished happily that the Irish Sea might be particularly choppy this day, and that Lord Melville had had a hearty breakfast.

The last Fencibles crossed, and the colonel spurred his horse to take the head of the column again. Anson came in behind the rear rank, set his sticks above his drum, and then froze at the bold-printed words of the broadside plastered on the bridge wall.

---

| **WANTED** | *and* | **WANTED** |
| --- | --- | --- |
| *For Sedition and Incitement to Rebellion* | | *For the Most Heinous Attack on and Murder of One of* |
| **OWEN ROE SULLIVAN** | | *His Majesty's* |
| *Also known as* | | *Loyal Staffordshire Fencibles* |
| *Owen Roe O'Sullivan* | | **RODERICK LEARY** |
| *Styled a Hedge Master* | | *Also known as Roderick O'Leary* |

*A Reward of £100 Sterling is Offered for*
*the Capture of Either by*
*Sir Parsons Melville, Lord of Melville, Ballyfin and Rushall*

---

His drumsticks still held in midair, Anson read and reread the broadside, then started at the clump of Sergeant Eyre's huge hand across his shoulder.

"Never mind about that. To your duty, Drummer. No, it's your duty you're to mind."

Anson felt his own stomach tighten and heave. Striding quickly beside Sergeant Eyre, he crossed the bridge—at its peak he could see the *Bonaventure* under light sail heading out into the bay—and took up his position by the Fencibles, drumming them in to New Barracks in time for the noon mess.

But Anson could not eat. He went instead to Colonel Staplyton's quarters, knocking louder than he had intended at the door.

When it opened, Anson saw that the colonel's face was indeed beaming. "Drummer," he called, as though delighted with his appearance, "you've caught me about to sit down to a bevy of dispatches, and I am eager to attend to none of them. Not under perfect skies such as these. Have you ever noticed, boy, how a spring day in Ireland can sometimes call to mind Gadshall? The green of it can be just the same."

"I have noticed, sir. But it's not about Gadshall that I've come."

The colonel shook his head. "I've not lived there one day in five since I attained this rank. But there are some nights when I could swear the breeze that puffs in the window has come fresh from Gadshall itself. I can almost hear your mother's voice upon it."

"Sir, there are broadsides posted for the capture of the hedge master, and for Roderick O'Leary."

"Roderick Leary," corrected the colonel. "There are indeed such broadsides."

"May I inquire, sir, how it was determined that Roderick O'Leary was responsible for the attack on Corporal Oakes and myself?"

"You may not inquire." Abruptly, the colonel's face was no longer beaming. "Certainly you do not believe, Drummer, that your commanding officer need reveal his investigative sources to one far inferior in rank."

"I understand that, sir. But may I ask, sir, if I was followed on the day I went on leave?"

"You may not ask that."

The colonel walked across the room and sat down at his desk. He laid his hand on top of the pile of dispatches. "Anson, you are putting me out of my humor."

"I am sorry for that, sir, but you must realize that Sorcha O'Leary will believe that it was I who gave Roderick's name to you."

"Why should you mind what Sorcha Leary believes?"

"I gave her my word, sir, on my honor as a Fencible, that I would not reveal it was her brother who threw the stones."

"It was a most inconvenient giving, Drummer. Most

inconvenient and inexpedient, putting you in the awkward situation of having to follow two loyalties."

"I understand that, sir."

"I do not believe you do. I do not believe you have for quite some time now. The loyalty of a Fencible, in addition to being unquestioned, is singular. It is not to be shared. It is not to be breached. It is not to be bandied with."

"And all this I have followed."

"You have not. You have withheld the name I sought out of misplaced honor. You have, Anson—do not trouble to deny it. You have kept faith with the Learys at the expense of the Fencibles."

"Their name is O'Leary."

The colonel sighed deeply. "You see how far your loyalty is breached."

"Sorcha will certainly believe that of me."

"She will be wrong. You have kept your loyalty with her quite well, and I have found other means to find the information I needed. The kind of information demanded by the king."

"And by Lord Melville."

"And by the family of Corporal Oakes himself." The colonel softened and leaned forward across his desk. "Anson, I have not questioned you on these matters, though such questioning was more than warranted. You were seen in the company of Owen Roe Sullivan, the hedge master. You were in attendance at his school. Is this not so?"

"It is, sir. I had not anticipated being spied upon."

"Am I to understand by that statement, Drummer, that you are loyal only when there is the possibility that you might be spied upon?"

"No, sir."

"I should think not. You do realize that the hedge schools, as they are called, are violations of the king's law?"

"I do, sir."

"And you chose not to report it to me. Or to take any action."

Silence from Anson. He felt like a child back at Staplyton Manor, alone and guilty before the great god of his father, whose perfect self looked down from on high to judge the imperfections of his runty son.

The colonel waited.

"Sir," said Anson slowly, quietly, "the hedge master's students read Latin. They speak their old tongue and they tell their old stories. There is such a music to it, such a rightness to it in that place. They do not offend against the king. They threaten no Fencible."

"Corporal Oakes might disagree with you." The colonel stood. "When we first stepped onto this green land, it was as beautiful a place as anyone could imagine. But it was a place at war, Anson, at constant, unending war. Tribe against tribe, family against family, petty king against petty king. There was no trade, no medicine, no learning, no organized agriculture. But now, hardly a day goes by without Irish corn, flax, wool, cattle, hams, tallow, barley flowing back in a flood to England. This is what the Fencibles have done. And Ireland will be the stronger for it. A decade from now the north shore of the Liffey will see some of the greatest building in all the realm."

"But at some cost, sir."

"Good God, Drummer, of course there is cost. No one who has lived here as long as I and seen this land, this place, can be blind to that. But Drummer, what you do not see is what might come of it all."

The colonel sat down, red faced. "In the end, Drummer, these are state matters, and not matters that call for your attention—or your meddling."

"Sir, the honor of a Fencible—"

"The honor of a Fencible is for his commanding officer to determine."

To this there was no answer. Anson stared at his father and found in the jut of his jaw, the scowl on his face, the intense belief in his own rightness a mirror of Lord Melville. He wondered, suddenly, if he looked the same to his father. The thought startled him, and he took a step back in a surprising fear.

"Sir, I will be late to the mess."

"I have one more question for you, Drummer, and here I beg the courtesy of a truthful answer."

"You will have it, sir."

"Answer me this: Did you know of the attack on Lord Melville's demesne?"

"Not until I saw the rising smoke, sir."

"You did not know of it prior to that time?"

"I did not."

A long pause. "Anson, if you had known of the coming attack, would you have warned me of it?"

"Is that why I have been taken off patrol, sir?"

"You are evasive. Answer the question."

It was a difficult task, since Anson himself was not sure of the answer. Would he have warned the Fencibles of an attack on Lord Melville? Surely. Would he have warned them if the warning meant the capture of the hedge master? Less surely. Would he have warned them if it meant the eviction of the O'Learys?

But under the terrible glare of his father, Anson quailed. He found himself pushed to a betrayal he did not accept yet could not deny. "Sir," he said quietly, "I believe I would have warned you of such an attack."

Colonel Staplyton nodded slowly. "I too believe you would have warned us. There is too much Fencible blood in you to do anything but your duty. You are dismissed to mess, Drummer."

"And the matter of the patrols, sir?"

"Dismissed, Drummer," growled the colonel.

The early-afternoon drills were lighthearted and giddy,

with Lord Melville safely away on the *Bonaventure*. Sergeant Eyre reversed the order of march again and again to see how many he could wrongfoot. Then he split the regiment in two and had them march with opposing strides, confusing Anson's rhythms. Then he had them march straight into each other, ending the afternoon drill in a roaring, guffawing cataclysm of red coats and rifles and stepped-on toes and askew hats.

But Anson could not be part of the guffaws. And he could not let Sorcha believe that he had betrayed her. He could not. Throughout the drill, he felt her hand in his, felt in the backs of his legs the descent through the furze, saw the tears on her cheeks at the tale of Tara.

And perhaps Sergeant Eyre understood all this when Anson came to him after drill to beg leave for the afternoon. The sergeant smiled but he shook his head.

"But I'll be back before evening mess, sir."

"I'm sure you would, Drummer. And I'm sure I would find all well when you rode up again. But with Dundrum and now Lord Melville's demesne, I'll not be letting any Fencible out alone."

"Then, sir, might I suggest that after today's drill, a ride with you in the countryside . . ."

"Now, Drummer," warned the sergeant.

"A ride in the spring air, with the scent of heather so thick you can hardly breath . . ."

"It is hardly fair to tempt a man."

"And perhaps a frothy cider at some cottage. The cider in Ireland, I hear, is finer than any you'll find in England."

Sergeant Eyre considered for a time, glancing only once toward to the colonel's office. "You're assigned to patrol this day," he said, "and the cider best be frothy."

So once more to the familiar road, this time with Sergeant Eyre. They passed the way to Lord Melville's demesne and the high hills from which Corporal Oakes was attacked. Along the way the air was indeed thick with heather, and Anson had no trouble urging the sergeant to a gallop. But when at last they looked down on the farmhouse where the air still smelled of the peat fire and goats still poked about the yard, Sergeant Eyre could hardly help but point out that two Fencibles were unlikely to get a frothy cider from the cottage of the Learys.

Still, Anson spurred his mount down and Sergeant Eyre followed. "Drummer, you'll like as not get dishwater—no cider here!" They clattered into the farmyard and Anson leaped down. "Sorcha," he called. "Sorcha O'Leary!"

But it was not Sorcha O'Leary who answered. A stocky, squat man opened the farmhouse door. He tilted his head to one side and peered at them suspiciously. "Should the Fencibles have business here?" he called. "Should the Fencibles not have business here, they had best be off."

Anson stood by the side of his horse, surprised and not a little fearful. "Where are the O'Learys?"

"The O'Learys ben't here anymore."

"Back on your horse, Anson," said Sergeant Eyre softly.

But Anson would not mount yet. "How could they not be here anymore?" he challenged.

"'Victed," said the squat man. "'Victed, that's all there is to the telling of it. And us given the place."

Anson remembered Sorcha's fear. Without their father and older brother, the O'Learys would not be able to work the land to a profit. And if Lord Melville knew that Roderick O'Leary had thrown the stones, he would certainly evict them. "Do you know where they've gone?" asked Anson eagerly. "Have they gone into Dublin?"

"Now how would I have the knowing of that?" said the man. "Leave Fencible matters to Fencibles is what I always say. So I'll do the leaving of it."

Anson looked up past the farmhouse, as though Sorcha would somehow appear on the heights, waving to him. But he could not even see the heights, so thick was the mist that rolled upon them. Anson turned back to the horse to hide the tears of frustration that sprang unexpectedly to his eyes.

"We'll be leaving then," called Sergeant Eyre, but Anson could not leave. He set one foot in the stirrup, but then swiped at his eyes and turned back to the farmhouse. Once he left this place, he would never be back, and the pelting sadness of that idea left him almost breathless.

Sergeant Eyre mounted. "We're to Dublin," he called. "Drummer, mount up."

Back on the road, Anson gave his mount her head. Her iron-clad hooves gutted the road.

And Sergeant Eyre rode behind slowly.

# CHAPTER

## 9

*T*hree days after Lord Melville's departure, Colonel Staplyton read new dispatches from London, then sent for his drummer to conduct Lieutenants Brockle and Fielding to his quarters. At their entrance, the colonel signed for Anson to remain, and he stood rigidly at attention. He was glad that he had checked his leggings and found them perfect.

"It seems, gentlemen," the colonel said slowly, "that the king is not altogether pleased with my handling of the Irish policy. He urges more resolute action and calls for a show of force and strength that would quell even the thought of an uprising."

"Sir, this has Lord Melville's hand upon it."

"More than his hand, Lieutenant Fielding, I should say."

"And yet, sir," said Lieutenant Brockle, "government

must have in mind the need to make examples to avoid future catastrophe."

"Indeed," agreed the colonel, "the king has examples much on his mind. There is mention here most especially of a young boy with chalk you may both remember." The colonel picked up one of the papers on his desk. "This dispatch suggests that hanging or at least the lash would have deterred similar assaults."

"So I suggested at the time, sir," said Lieutenant Brockle.

"I recall it." The colonel walked across the room and watched the drills in the quadrangle. Anson shifted his eyes—he kept his head perfectly steady—to watch his father. Clearly the drills pleased him. It was something Anson felt as well. The perfect precision of a turning regiment, the alignment of men and equipment: These were the essential guts of the empire that brought peace and security to the world.

The colonel shook his head and turned back to the lieutenants. "Gentleman, I have marched across French battlefields through air so thick with lead balls that I could ring my saber against them. And now I am advised to hang an Irish child."

"But merely as an example, sir."

"One does not hang examples, Lieutenant Brockle." The colonel took a rolled dispatch from his desk, paused a moment, then handed it to the lieutenant. "But such matters may be far from your mind, now. You will find a matter of interest to you here. You are promoted to captain."

"Sir, I never expected—"

"You have a new patron, Brockle."

"I believe I may enjoy the happiness of such, sir. It would be difficult to rise in the world without one. Most particularly in Ireland, where officers are banished from friends and relations and all hope of preferment."

"Indeed. Well, you will have certain matters to attend. I wish you joy of your promotion, Captain. Dismissed."

"Thank you, sir."

Captain Brockle turned smartly and stepped out of the colonel's quarters. Anson kept his eyes straight ahead, but he stood no more rigidly than Lieutenant Fielding, who was still at attention.

"You have nothing to say, Lieutenant?"

"Nothing, sir."

"You have no complaint to make, though this appointment passes you over?"

"None, sir."

The colonel sighed, nodding his head. "Then might I ask you, Lieutenant, to have a horse saddled for me within the quarter hour?"

"Your destination, sir?"

"I would see this dangerous Dublin for myself. I would

see if the whole of British foreign policy rests upon one child with a piece of chalk."

"You'll remember, sir, that no Fencible is to leave New Barracks unaccompanied. And no Fencible is to be unarmed. Your own orders, sir."

The colonel turned to Anson. "I wonder, Lieutenant, if the drummer might know of a Fencible who would be willing to accompany his commanding officer."

"I expect he might," said the Lieutenant.

Anson could not stop himself. He let his eyes drift to his father's face. What he saw there was something he had always hoped for and rarely found. Pleasure. Unalloyed pleasure. "Sir," said Anson quietly, "if it would not be inappropriate . . ."

"It would not," finished the colonel, "despite the one smudge on the left legging."

Within the quarter hour Colonel Staplyton and Anson—who had cleaned the smudge from his left legging—had left New Barracks, crossed the Liffey, and were riding along the bay. The sea showed itself gray and white until the wind troubled it into purple and, almost, a deep black. When the sun eked a shaft through the overhang, a patch would turn to a bright green. Through all these changes, a grouping of silent guillemots rose and fell, rose and fell, rose and fell with each of the waves blown across the Irish Sea. They seemed buoyed and eternal.

The colonel looked out to the water and then back to the rolling heather behind. "They call this the land of Tir na n-Og, the Land of the Ever Young. Maybe it is indeed. Must you look so surprised, Drummer?" The colonel laughed, the hearty laugh of joyousness.

"I had no notion, sir, that you knew anything of the Irish stories."

"A colonel sent to command a regiment outside his own country had best know as much of the country he is to subdue as he might." He pointed down to the spit of land that stuck its tongue out to taste the salt of the Irish Sea. "Sea campion there, then thrift and squill. And that curious plant there, that seems to turn back upon itself in that melancholy way—bird's-foot trefoil."

Colonel Staplyton turned again to the ocean. "By God, Anson, look at it. The first racehorses in Ireland came from mares brought down to that very coast and left there for the sea horses to visit. Their colts ran with the swiftness of the waves."

Below them the tide had drawn out, and men with jackets the color of the rocks bent over the open underside of the sea, gathering the seaweed that would make their gardens fertile. Donkeys with baskets stood patiently, sniffing at the salt ground as soggy weed was loaded armful by armful onto their backs, each load pressing the water out of the load below it. One young boy stood by the head of his donkey as his father loaded, and when he began to sing a clear tune, it sounded as if the sea itself had composed it, and the men with their weeds unbent and listened.

"Tir na n-Og," whispered the colonel. He looked to Anson. "Boy, I had thought it would always be the battlefield that would keep me ever young. But there is no battlefield here. I send my patrols through the city, and if a report comes in of a still brought over from France, I send a squad to a coast or bogland to capture a smuggler and spill his spirits into the peat. By God, there's a victory for you. And now I am to hang little boys." Suddenly he was no longer joyous.

"Sir," said Anson, "let me take you to Phoenix Park. It will bring to mind Gadshall itself. You'll feel as if you are walking in the fields past Staplyton Manor." The colonel nodded as though very tired.

They rode without speaking back into the city, passing the north quays one by one. Many who saw them looked away, some with curled lips. But others—those whose families had not lived in Dublin long enough for them to have lost the English edge of their tongues—tipped their hats to them. Each time the colonel lowered his head, they smiled at the return.

"The God of heaven love you," a shopkeeper called to him, waddling out with a mug of ale. "To you and yours, Colonel. Throw it back in you." The colonel reached down from his mount and took the drink in a single draft, earning the cheers of the shopkeeper.

"The finest ale north or south of the Liffey, was it not, Colonel?"

"The very finest," answered Colonel Staplyton.

"And one for the boy, then?"

The colonel looked at Anson. "One for the boy." And when the shopkeeper ran as best he could to fetch the ale, the colonel whispered, "Charity, Anson." Anson knew why when he drank the ale. It was not the finest north or south of the Liffey. One could hardly imagine it being the finest anywhere.

"Indeed," cried Anson, "I've never had its like before."

"And never will again," agreed the shopkeeper.

At the corner of Capel Street, the colonel reined back his mount for an old woman who had trundled herself out of a shop and stepped in front of the horse, almost under his very hooves. With a snort, the horse shied, and the woman looked up, sheepish at the commotion. "Wisha, God bless you," she called to the colonel.

"And you too, madam."

"And is that your son, then, behind you, looking for all the world like a young colonel his own self?"

"It is."

She peered long at Anson, the smile deep in her eyes. "Don't they carry the future of the world, then?" she said to the colonel.

Colonel Staplyton turned and looked at Anson, and for

a long time they stared into each other. "Yes, they do," said the colonel finally, as if discovering something for the very first time. "They do indeed carry the future of the world."

It seemed almost a holiday to Anson, riding along the quays. Though the sky still hung dark and the river swirled as if something were troubling it just below its surface, Anson hardly noticed, if he noticed at all. He could not remember a time when he and his father had ever moved in companionable silence, and the almost physical pleasure of it surprised him into a grin. This, combined with the freedom from New Barracks and the sense that Dublin was not so dangerous a place after all, made him want to set his mare to a gallop, to race his father through the cobbled streets and have neither outpace the other.

They dismounted at Phoenix Park, tied their mounts to a post, and strolled in, Anson ahead and urging his father to the beauties of the place: the herd of grazing deer that would almost suffer a touch, the cropped fields of meadow grass that molded themselves to ripples like the sea, the ancient oaks that had seen Fencibles come and go for more than a century, the stone walls softened by moss that looked for all the world like those of Gadshall.

At first the colonel walked with his hands clasped sedately behind his back. But soon his pace quickened as he followed Anson deeper into the park, deeper and still deeper until Dublin seemed left behind and they were together again in earlier days. Anson could imagine that his sisters and mother would come out with a basket lunch from behind that grove of aspens.

"It is Gadshall," said the colonel eagerly. "It is its like. Now if only the sun were to come out and strike just so . . ."

And at just that moment, as if Ireland itself heard them, the sun did come out, and it did strike just so, and Anson and his father clapped each other on the shoulders in awe and laughter and delight at the full perfection of the moment. Even when the clouds pinched themselves together again to hide the light, they could still feel the warm beam of that warm moment in the country of Tir na n-Og.

Farther into Phoenix Park, so that now even the sounds of Dublin were so faint that Anson could not decide if what he heard were the bells and clattering of the city or the wind rattling the rhododendrons. Farther down a tree-shaded path, whose bends led them to the groin of two hills, the bottom boggy with dark pools and low myrtles. And then up again and closer to the water, past the glossy ferns atwitter with wrens, and suddenly out into the open, where piles of rocks perched uneasily one upon the other, their silver lichens catching what light there was like the dust of coins. Farther and still farther, to where the rocks thinned out until they might have been giant playthings left behind on the moor, while birches looked on and groomed their lovely hair.

Past the birches, the River Liffey ran jauntily beside the lowlands, marked here and there by floating lilies and the silver-gray backs of wild geese. And beyond the river, fields lay brown under the sky. One still held last season's cornstalks, these being investigated by a flock of mallards, who toppled in and out of the water as if they could not for the life of them decide where to dwell.

"Lieutenant Fielding will be pacing if we are to linger much longer," said the colonel.

"And Sergeant Eyre have me by the ear," added Anson.

"Then to save Fielding's soles and your lobes, we had best be off."

One last look, and then their backs to the moors and the river. Past the strewn boulders, and then down between the hills again, down where the trees drew shade about themselves like skirts and the mosses grew thick and quiet.

Too quiet. Not a single wren twittered.

And then six men stepped out. Darker than the darkness, they stood with legs wide, bludgeons smacking against their palms, caps pulled low over their foreheads.

"Dundrum," growled one.

"Your sword, Drummer!" cried the colonel. But before Anson had fully drawn it out, they were upon them with battering blows.

Lieutenant Fielding was indeed pacing, and though the soles of his boots were not in immediate danger, the carpet in Colonel Staplyton's quarters was. Up and down he paced, up and down, up and down, until Captain Brockle roared at him to halt.

"Sir, they've been gone more than their allotted time."

"And you propose to do what, Lieutenant?" Captain Brockle stressed the last word. He fingered the new horn buttons on his spatterdashes.

"A patrol, sir, to find them."

"A fine fool I should look if on the first day of my command, I should send a patrol running madly about Dublin for two dawdling Fencibles."

Lieutenant Fielding leaned over the desk behind which Captain Brockle sat. "Brockle, you are aware of the state of Dublin. There are some who would find the sight of the colonel and his son too much the target to ignore."

"I know of no such thing, and the address is 'Captain.'"

"Then, Captain, I formally request that a patrol be sent . . ."

"Request denied. I have not the men nor the leisure to . . . Lieutenant, you have not been dismissed. Nor will you turn your back to me without appropriate salute. Lieutenant, a salute, do you hear?"

Outside, Lieutenant Fielding spat viciously on the cobbles of the quadrangle. "There's your salute, you bastard," he muttered, then bellowed for Sergeant Eyre. It would be worth his life, said the lieutenant, to have a mount saddled directly. Sergeant Eyre understood, and in a shorter time than the lieutenant had any right to expect, the sergeant returned with two mounts, a saber at his own belt.

"I asked for a single mount, Sergeant."

"Colonel Staplyton's orders, sir. No man is to leave New Barracks—"

"Yes, Sergeant, and might I suppose you would ride after me even should I give the order to stay?"

"You might suppose that, sir."

"Then we shall avoid having you taken up on charges."

"Thank you, sir. And not that I'd pretend to lead, sir, but the drummer has shown himself to be most partial to Phoenix Park."

"My thought precisely, Sergeant." They rode out in a cascade of hooves, saluting briskly toward the colonel's quarters.

The Colonel and Anson had driven back the first attack easily, keeping the bludgeons from reaching their skulls with the slashing of their sabers. Every feint the men made, every quick and aborted charge, Anson followed easily. The points of the two Staplyton sabers flashed so quickly through the air that they were always perched at the heart of the nearest attacker, who would flinch back, appalled. Once Anson lunged forward as if to drive the attackers away all by himself, and he felt his saber slide into the living sinews of a man, a sliding that made all his blood retreat. But in the lunge, he had opened both flanks, and though he dodged the first bludgeon, only the colonel's shout and own lunge had kept him from more than a glancing blow on the left shoulder.

While two men carried their wounded comrade to a safe distance down the path, the others stared at the Staplytons as demons might. When they renewed their attack, they had clearly thought of a strategy. "Anson," whispered the colonel, "they'll be turning both flanks and encircling us. As they circle, wheel and face until we are back to back. Understand? Wheel and face. If only this ground were surer footing, I'd order retreat, but they'd be upon us as quick as thought."

"No need to retreat, sir. One of them is already down, and we've got two good swords and each other."

The colonel turned to face Anson. "By God, we do," he said.

Then the attack came again, and Anson wheeled and faced. He felt, rather than saw, the colonel's struggle behind him. He heard the rip of a sword through the air, the grunts of the colonel as he lunged, the scraping of his boots against rock as he tried to tear away the moss for a surer footing. He knew for a certainty that the colonel could not, would not be breached, that the attackers might as well have tried to carve granite with spoons if they hoped to get at his back.

The thought determined Anson to be the same for his father. Though this time the attackers came side by side, Anson was always able to swipe one to a retreat and then whisk his point to the other, so that soon he had tattered the coats of two men and bloodied one. "It will take more than blood to drown away the sin of Dundrum," the attacker said, menacing. Anson knew that his father would never have answered, so he held his sword before him with silent and grim certainty.

Then a sudden rush, and with a cry Anson felt his swordpoint go deep into the attacker who wanted more than blood. But he could not jerk the point out and elbow it around before the second was upon him, striking at his forearm so that his sword fell. A second bludgeon to his neck, and he was knocked down with the force of it, struggling against the darkness that threatened to engulf his eyes. A kick in the chest, and Anson felt his ribs creak and almost yield. A weight astride him, a confused sight of a raised forearm, and then a shriek that would startle the banshees, a horrid gurgle of a sound that did not end even after the weight toppled from his chest. It slithered into an airy groan, and then silence.

Anson propped himself up on an elbow and tried desperately to wipe away the red cloud that hovered deep in his eyeballs. As though looking through a sunset, he saw the mountain of his father heaved up between himself and the remaining attackers. He still erupted into attacks with the efficient mastery of a Fencible, but his left arm hung crookedly, and the side of his head—when had his hair turned so silver?—was bright with red. Anson blinked, then blinked again, groping about for his sword and finally finding it under the corpse that no longer shrieked. He rose to one knee, shaking his head to scuttle the cloud, then rose shakily, spreading his legs wide and holding his arms out for balance.

And then he heard the quick sizzle of burning powder, the *thunk* of a contained explosion, and the rip of a lead bullet down a barrel.

"Aren't those Fencible mounts?" asked Sergeant Eyre, pointing over the open acres of the park.

Lieutenant Fielding did not answer but spurred his horse savagely, so that even as she jumped to a gallop, she whinnied with the pain of it.

They were indeed Fencible mounts, most certainly those of the colonel and drummer. Sergeant Eyre scrambled down to grab their halters.

"They would hardly have left them here to graze untethered," said Lieutenant Fielding thoughtfully, looking about him. "And if they had, they would have stayed within eyesight."

Sergeant Eyre held up the leads of the two horses. "Sir, these horses have been loosed." Quickly he led them to a row of aspens and secured them, then remounted and followed the lieutenant, who had already started to skirt the open meadow to find a path that might lead into the woods.

"Damn the thickness of the place," cried Lieutenant Fielding. "They might have gone any way, not even taken a path."

"In that case, sir, one way is as good as another."

"Indeed. Sergeant, you take the north side, I the south. Follow the first path that leads in. God help them if they are to be ambushed in a place such as this."

And then came the shot, a perfect, clear singularity in the welter of a thousand wooded acres.

"I believe that God has just helped them, sir," shouted the sergeant. They pricked their horses to a gallop along the wood's edge, gathering them in an upheaval of horse and rider at a path that cut in, and pushing them recklessly over such slippery ground as no horse will take without shying. But even the horses had caught the wild emergency of the ride, and they clattered with mostly sure feet over sliding slate and moss-dampened stones, catching themselves when a foreleg went out. The riders gripped the manes so that they might not fall over their horses' dipping heads.

They raged through clearings like maddened plows and crashed through thickening trees like the roll of an avalanche. Slicing twigs tore at their faces as they passed, but they could not spare a hand to shield themselves as the horses rollicked from side to side, one moment at full gallop, the next shuffling for a footing. When the path began to leap down like a stream, each rounded stone threatening a topple, the horses spread and braced their back legs, kept their heads low, and abandoned themselves to the descent, rushing down in a great flow of rock and grit and branches until they came to the flat bottom, where they pressed into a lathering gallop and burst into the shadows that eclipsed the afternoon.

The rocky, clattering, sparking outrage of their approach must have been heard by fully half of County Dublin. But what with the shrieks and curses that flew from both Anson and the men whose hands and faces burned from the scalpel cuts he gave, none of those still battling in the darkened woods heard the riders. They came down on such a sudden that they could not stop their horses from galloping over the man whom Anson had first wounded, and who had just finished reloading and taking aim at the Fencible still standing over the fallen colonel. It was his shriek, and the fearsome battle cry gutting out from Sergeant Eyre's ancestral past, that turned the other three away from the wide sweeps Anson was using to hold them back from his father.

It seemed as if an entire troop of Fencibles had appeared. One of the attackers turned and threw his bludgeon wildly at Anson, then leaped with the others to the darker woods. He crashed ahead just in front of Sergeant Eyre, who had jumped like a warrior from his mount and was rampaging after them. The choking screams that came back to Anson were terrible to hear.

When Sergeant Eyre returned with set face and bloody sword, he found Anson and the lieutenant bent over the colonel. He set his hand on Anson's shoulder and nodded to him.

"Damnation, Lieutenant, it is just a ball," said the colonel hoarsely. "As if you and I hadn't had more than one in and out of us before this time." He spoke slowly, with short gaspy breathes.

"But this is a ball, sir, that strikes awfully close to—"

"There are times, Lieutenant, when I regret your father was a surgeon." He coughed one, twice, and spat up a spot of blood. "Anson," the colonel called.

Anson put his arm across his father's chest. "Here, sir."

"You did well, boy. Well. Just that one breach, and that quickly closed. If it had not been for the one villain with the musket, we would have driven them off."

"We would, sir."

"The wide strokes toward the end, to cover me. That was properly done. You did not learn that from me."

"No, sir. It is a stroke Sergeant Eyre has drilled."

"Then," said the colonel, coughing again, "you will remember a pint pot of cool ale for the man. Draw it from the regimental stores when we return."

"I will, sir."

The colonel nodded and closed his eyes.

"We need to lift him astride my horse," whispered

Lieutenant Fielding. "Anson, you bring her around. And for God's sake, Sergeant, be gentle."

"As gentle as my own mother, sir."

"Anson, that low ground will do for the mare. Once your father is astride, take the other mount and fetch the carriage from New Barracks. And now, Colonel, with your pardon." But the colonel gave no response.

Aghast, Anson winded his horse. Ignoring the cries of Captain Brockle, he fitted the carriage and bolted back to Phoenix Park. When he drew the lathering horse to a halt, the sergeant and lieutenant were just leading the mare out of the wood, her mane darkly stained with the bright blood of Colonel Staplyton's left lung.

CHAPTER

# 10

*A*nson, his chest bare but for the wide bandage that spanned his bruised ribs, stood with his arms held somewhat painfully out from his sides. "Mending well," Dr. Hoccleve said, running his thick fingers up Anson's side and pushing, Anson thought, as if he knew exactly where it would hurt the most. "You might have been stove in, and nearly were. Does it pain?"

"Not in the least, sir."

"Your face declares you a liar, Drummer. Be gone and tend to the colonel."

Anson eased himself into his shirt and returned to his father, who had now been lying in the infirmary at New Barracks for most of a week, unconscious with the morphine elixir that, Dr. Hoccleve said, might allow him to heal. It was a troubled rest, filled with bouts of wasting sweats and delirious returns to old battlefields. But at least now the colonel no longer bloodied the sheets with his spittle, and Anson, who had stroked his silver hair to set it in place, thought he might be breathing without quite the fluttery rasp that had marked his first three nights.

Yet he did not open his eyes. And he did not answer to his name. And he did not press Anson's hand in return.

Anson settled himself down on the stool beside his father. He would stay there again this night and hope that he would wake himself early enough to drum in the muster. Yawning, he stretched until his ribs hurt, then took off his coat in the heat of this place. He would put it on again just after evening mess, when Lieutenant Fielding came off duty and visited the colonel.

Anson wondered—as he had wondered many times these last days—where Sorcha and Roddy had gone. And whether the hedge master was with them. He imagined them huddled in a peaty cave, their hands held out to the smallest of fires, the sweet smoke of the turf blowing out in tiny wisps through the tufts of heather that covered the entrance. Maybe they set their backs against the dead cold of a stone slab. Maybe there was only the peat. He could see the hedge master fussing over a troublesome translation of Virgil, holding it low to catch some light of the fire. Perhaps he had set a passage of Augustine for Roddy.

And Sorcha. He could see Sorcha with her hair pulled tight under a kerchief, her face smudged a bit. Her dark eyes held the ruddy glow of the embers.

Anson folded his coat over the back of the chair, then

leaned into it until he found a position where no buttons bored into him. He yawned again and closed his eyes. He wondered if Sorcha was warm. He wondered if she had a coat.

And then he was asleep.

That was how Lieutenant Fielding found him, as he had found him most every night since he had carried the colonel to the infirmary. The lieutenant pressed his hand against the colonel's brow and gently smoothed out his blankets. Then he draped a blanket around Anson's shoulders—here he could be as rough as he pleased, since the boy never woke—and left. He was due in Captain Brockle's quarters.

When Lieutenant Fielding entered, Captain Brockle sat behind Colonel Staplyton's desk. He did not look up, and the lieutenant had a moment to run his finger around the collar of his uniform. The quarters were overheated; Captain Brockle liked it that way. Sergeant Eyre, who stood at attention beside him, did not.

Captain Brockle had laid out the map of Dublin and the surrounding towns on the desk. "Tomorrow, Sergeant, you'll concentrate the patrols at the Stony Batter here, and here."

"Yes, sir."

"You will search each of the houses along this street. Search them thoroughly. Confiscate any weapons, any papers that might be of interest. Arrest those who resist."

"Yes, sir. Sir, begging your pardon, but you should know that these searches have put the whole of Dublin into a stew. And the search yesterday at Malahide, sir, why it turned into a looting rout. Half the men who came back with you were drunk, and the other half stuffed to the gills with whatever they might carry. The colonel would never countenance it, sir."

Captain Brockle stood up abruptly.

"The colonel is not in command, nor will he be in command until he recovers fully. Until such time, Sergeant, I will carry out my orders as I see fit, and the orders that I have are from the king himself."

"From Lord Melville more like, if you pardon me, sir."

"Sergeant, you are insubordinate. Too insubordinate by far. It is the king who demands a firm hand, and he shall have it. Owen Roe Sullivan will be on a transport by the end of the month. And Roderick Leary cold in his grave."

Lieutenant Fielding cleared his throat hoarsely. "Permission to speak, sir."

"Denied. Sergeant, you have your orders. Dismissed." Sergeant Eyre threw a brisk and purposeful salute, then left.

Captain Brockle turned to a stack of documents, read through the first two, then set them slowly aside. "Lieutenant Fielding, the drummer has been off duty these six days."

"He has, sir. Tending to his father."

"He will be back on patrol tomorrow. He is a Fencible, not a convalescent nurse. See to it."

"Anything else, sir?"

Brockle looked at him sharply. Nothing that Lieutenant Fielding ever said could be interpreted as improper, but there was just that tinge of insolence that he would wipe out, if he could. "Lieutenant, I will be the one sending reports of your conduct back to London. Your continued career lies in these hands now."

Lieutenant Fielding stared straight ahead. He said nothing.

"Dismissed." A salute and Lieutenant Fielding was gone. The draft of cool air he left behind swirled around Captain Brockle's feet and up to his knees. He called to his aide for more coal.

At first light, Anson drummed the Fencibles to muster, ate a hurried mess, and marched at the head of three squadrons across the river and up to the Stony Batter. They marched quickly and silently, Anson's drumsticks in his pack. At the Batter, Sergeant Eyre sealed off either end of the street and called off the Fencibles who would search each of the houses along its length.

"The man I see with a drop of liquor in him," he threatened, "is the man who'll never taste another drop of it as long as he's a Fencible under my command. And as for looters . . ." Sergeant Eyre glared savagely at the ranks. There was no need to say anything more.

The searches began. Each of the houses spat its family out onto the street, some still in their bedclothes and all red faced. Some stood around disheveled and stricken, unsure of how it had come to pass that they were in the street and a patrol was rummaging through their houses. Neighbors gathered together in the center of the street, and the glares of impotent hatred that they speared at the Fencibles showed that King George had won no loyalties this day.

From one of the central houses, Anson saw, the Fencibles pushed out a tall older man. Had he been dressed and groomed, he would have been regarded as distinguished by any man in London itself. Now, however, skinny red legs stuck out to bare feet, and he hobbled gingerly about the cobblestones. His robe was on inside out, and he could not find the tie. He alternated between searching for it and holding the robe tight about him. His perfectly full and white hair, a striking feature, Anson thought, should he ever have his portrait done, sprawled in several shocks, so that he looked perpetually surprised.

In exasperation he flung his robe back and made his way to the end of the street, where Anson waited just behind Sergeant Eyre.

"And is this what His Majesty's subjects are to expect? Fencibles in their houses at an ungodly hour? Searches with no cause? And if it had been raining a flood, would you still have scattered us out of our beds?"

"I am under orders, sir," said Sergeant Eyre, slowly and almost ashamedly, as if resorting to the excuse of a scoundrel.

"Under orders? Whose orders, Sergeant?"

"Those of Captain Brockle."

"Are you not Staffordshire Fencibles? By God, Colonel Staplyton will hear of this outrage, sir. He would never countenance it."

"My own words exactly, sir. But the colonel is not currently in command, as you may have heard."

A cry from another house, and they all turned to see a Fencible being chased down its stoop by the broom-wielding mistress of the house, her hand so deft with the sweeping that she seemed to come at the Fencible from all sides at once. "Out, out!" she cried. "Are you mad, to think that you may come into an honest lady's house this hour of the morning? With her babies still asleep in their very cribs?"

Seeing the battle, two other women dashed back inside their own homes, and Anson could not tell if the shrieks that came out of their open doors were from the attacking women or the attacked Fencibles.

"So it has come to this," said the white-haired gentleman. "The Staffordshire Fencibles are battling the women of Ireland. Beware, Sergeant, lest your defeat be larger than you can imagine."

Anson looked up and down the Batter. The dark-yellow light of early morning had not dried off the tendrils of fog, and they reached around the ankles of the people standing in the street. He saw them shivering into each other. And then one young boy leaned down and picked up a stone. He held it purposefully in his palm.

"Sergeant Eyre," said Anson.

"I notice, Drummer. By God, I'll not be arresting boys for throwing stones this day of the world. Not when I would be doing the same if it were me there." Sergeant Eyre stood high in his stirrups. "Drummer," he barked, "sound the recall. The Stony Batter is clear."

Anson drew out his sticks and pounded out the recall, pattering out its rhythm perhaps a bit too quickly. It was only a few moments before the patrol had gathered together in formation again, then only another few moments before they were marching back to New Barracks. The stone was never thrown.

When Captain Brockle learned that Sergeant Eyre had returned with neither arms nor papers nor prisoners, he would not wait to summon him but surged out into the quadrangle like a torrent, scattering Fencibles from his roaring sides as easily as pebbles. The torrent swirled more and more fiercely, as the sergeant could not be found in the barracks, in the mess, even in the chapel. By the time Captain Brockle found the sergeant and drummer seated by the side of the unconscious colonel, the torrent had grown wild.

The sergeant and drummer stood to attention.

"By God, Sergeant, why did you not report?"

"I would have been on my way to you in just a moment, sir, but I would see if the colonel—"

"The condition of the colonel is the affair of Dr. Hoccleve. It is none of yours. Your duty, Sergeant, was to carry out my orders and then report to me. You did neither."

"Begging your pardon, sir, I—"

"Neither, Sergeant. Where are the prisoners you might have taken? And the arms? Do you think there isn't a soul in County Dublin who is not laughing at the Staffordshire Fencibles as we speak?"

"I know of at least one, sir," said the Sergeant evenly.

"Damn your incompetence. Sergeant, if you keep your present rank, it will be by grace alone. You may be assured of never rising higher."

Sergeant Eyre stared straight ahead. He said nothing.

"And you, boy, what are you about? Does your present duty assign you here?"

"It was me that offered to bring the boy to his father, sir," said the sergeant.

"Then, Drummer, you have followed bad counsel. A Fencible follows his duty, not his whims. Be glad I do not bend you over a railing myself. As God is my witness, boy, neither your name nor your connections would save you from it."

Anson decided that he too would remain silent.

Captain Brockle paced back and forth, his hands clasping and unclasping behind his back. "Sergeant," he said coming back to them, "call out the men for a search at dusk. I myself will lead to prevent another rout. You, boy, will sound the march as loudly as ever you can. We'll show Dublin that the king's Fencibles are not to be cowed. Sergeant, you will see to it that New Barracks is secure. You are able to see to that, are you not?"

"I am, sir."

"Then dismissed to your duties, both of you. And Drummer, you are to keep watch-and-watch until further notice. Sergeant, see to it." Captain Brockle followed the rest of his torrent out of the infirmary.

Sergeant Eyre blew out a long breath. "Well, young Staplyton, there's that."

Anson shrugged his shoulders, then turned back to his father. He leaned down and did something he did not remember ever doing before. He did it on a sudden impulse, with no embarrassment, no hesitation, as though he had done it all the days of his life. He kissed him gently on his forehead.

The search on the Lower Baggot that evening was nothing like that on the Stony Batter. After marching in great pomp and show on the north side of St. Stephen's Green, Anson clattering at his drum as loudly as ever he could, the Fencibles burst to a sudden assault on the Baggot, and those who had come out to see the display were sealed from their houses and could not go back in, no matter the sounds of smashed furniture and shivered glass. In the eerily moving light of torches held by the stern Fencibles, the people of the Lower Baggot stood sullen and more than a little hopeless. The first man who barred his house to the Fencibles saw its door crashed in; his wife saw him carried off as a rebel. Anson could still hear her weeping behind her ruined door.

Already tripods of confiscated muskets perched at the end of the street closest to the Green, where Captain Brockle waited on horseback, Anson standing beside him. A Fencible approached with a cache of papers, some with red wax seals that glowed dully in the torchlight. The captain reached down and took them eagerly, quickly rifling through them, then dashing them to the street. "Bills of sale, private. They are merely bills of sale." Anson could almost imagine that he heard Captain Brockle grinding his teeth. "It's information of Leary and Sullivan that we're about, not bills of sale." The private saluted and faded back into the darkness of the street. Anson thought that he would not return to the captain if he came upon the whereabouts of the Pope himself hiding on the Lower Baggot.

Then another Fencible appeared, and by the way Captain Brockle leaned forward in his saddle, Anson could see that here was something that interested him enormously. The Fencible dragged a young boy behind him, jerking him forward though the boy spread his heels against the cobblestones. Behind him came two more Fencibles, their muskets at the level and crossed in front of what must be the boy's parents, the mother leaning against the father, and the father holding a hand up to an eye. Anson could see even in the torchlight that the eye was already swelling.

"The boy with the chalk," said Captain Brockle slowly, and it sounded to Anson as though he were about to eat him. "Not so clever now."

"We had Colonel Staplyton's own assurance that this matter was at an end," cried the father.

"The attack on the colonel reopens this matter," returned Captain Brockle.

"My boy had nothing to do with that."

"Perhaps not. But there are matters that he might know of that do touch upon that attack. Perhaps they are matters that you yourself know of."

Silence from the two parents. From the boy, defiance. He stood straight, his face uplifted, ready to front all the armies of King George. Anson had seen the same haughtiness at the O'Leary farm, and he wondered if he would have been able to show it, if it was he caught in a Fencible grasp.

"I think I have what I want," said Captain Brockle, studying the faces of the boy's parents. "I'll take your boy for questioning this night. Come in the morning, if you'd do me the courtesy."

"Ask all the questions you'd like," cried the boy. "You'll be getting as much as would sod a lark."

"I think not," said the captain slowly, still eyeing the

silent father, the weeping mother. "Drummer, the recall," said Captain Brockle, and pulled his horse back around toward the green and New Barracks.

Anson began his first watch as soon as they arrived. Off at midnight, he was on again before dawn, and then again by midmorning. He would make no complaint, nor would he allow the sleepiness that pulled down at his shoulders to show itself to the captain. To stay awake, he watched two mounted squadrons organize their restless horses into ranks. He closed his eyes against the sparkle of their harness, then quickly opened them when he realized with a start that he was falling asleep even as he stood. He began to sweat and wondered if he would faint.

Then, across the quadrangle, the door to the colonel's quarters opened and the boy's parents came out under armed escort. The mother paced eagerly, and as they crossed, she looked past Anson and to the guardhouse behind him as though she could pierce through it with her very eyes. But the father walked slow and shamefaced, his eyes on the cobblestones of the quadrangle, his cap still in his hands, wringing it as if he would draw water from its wool.

"You'll wait here," announced the escort, and stifling a cry, the mother stopped, while the father kept at the wringing of his cap. Though Anson stood not three paces from them, they pretended not to see each other. But Anson could not be near her without thinking of his own mother, and how she would have stood at such a moment. She would not have let her tears show; there would certainly have been none of that. But he knew that her heart would have been churning within, and that once the crisis was over, she would have gone quietly, slowly, to her room, and then not appeared until morning, still red eyed.

The oak door of the brig swung open, and the mother gave a slight gasp. But it was only another Fencible, going about his duties with a great yawn, just another day like all other days.

The mother reached for the father's hand, and as if he were surprised at finding his cap where it was, he hurriedly slapped it on his head and held her. He glanced once at Anson, their eyes meeting for a moment, then looked back to the cobblestones.

The door opened again, and this time it was the boy, his shoulder grasped roughly by the escort. He raised one hand to shield his blinking eyes from the light and with the other reached out to his mother, who was already upon him, encircling him and putting herself between the Fencible and her son. He held on to her, but not like a small child who had been lost; more like a man who had come out the far end of a hard time and who was comforting someone who had been worrying back at home.

All the while, the father had not moved.

"Da," said the boy finally, "I'm all right, you see."

"The purveyance of God," he said, quietly nodding back.

"So there's naught you had to tell them."

"We'll be going away from this place, then," said the father, turning away.

"It's all like I told you," the boy said to the mother.

"Let's be getting you home," she answered, and taking him by the shoulders, she led him past the father, who walked slowly after them, stooped and swiping at his eyes. He looked up only once, as the mounted Fencibles swept past them and out the gates of New Barracks. The mother turned back to look at her husband, then held her son all the tighter as they too went out the gates.

Two watches later, after Anson had just dragged himself away from the guardhouse and was falling into a dead sleep, he half heard the squadrons returning. For a moment, he thought he might go to see them ride in, but he had been on watch-and-watch through the night and day, and the bunk was so comfortable, even though it was just a bunk, and he was on the edge of a delicious dream, and . . . So he was asleep.

It was not long enough. It never was, for someone on watch-and-watch, pulling himself up every four hours through the livelong day. A touch from Sergeant Eyre on his shoulder, since the hours had run faster than they had any right to, and Anson started, groaned once as his body rebelled at the notion of rising again, then pushed himself past the dizziness of sleep into something like consciousness. He dressed, gathered the musket—unloaded; Sergeant Eyre had seen to it—and with half-closed eyes walked back to the guardhouse. He tripped over a cobblestone once, then resolved that Captain Brockle, should he be looking out over the quadrangle, should not see him falter. He squared his shoulders, stifled the great yawn that wanted to retch its way out of his gullet, and proceeded to the guardhouse as a Fencible should.

Lieutenant Fielding was waiting for him, his face drawn and stern, for all the world as if he had just come from a battle. "Drummer," he said formally, "you'll be inside, stationed hard by the cell door. I'll assign the outside duty to someone else."

"Yes, sir. There's a prisoner then?"

"Indeed," said the lieutenant stiffly, "there is a prisoner." Perhaps Anson was imagining it, but suddenly he was sure that if he turned about quickly, he would find that the eyes of Captain Brockle were in fact assessing his back. "You'll be concerned about your father. Dr. Hoccleve will be here directly to attend to the prisoner, and I'll ask him to bring a report to you."

"Yes, sir. Thank you, sir."

"Anson," began the lieutenant. Though his face kept its granite hardness, his tone relaxed some into familiarity.

"Anson, should your father—That is, I believe that you should know that—" He paused, his mouth working.

"Thank you, sir," said Anson quietly. "I've come to know it." Lieutenant Fielding nodded, then turned quickly away to his duties.

Anson stepped into the guardhouse, glad of the wooden door between himself and Captain Brockle's eyes. It was a perfectly square room, as solid as it was simple. There were no windows. There was nothing on the floor but a scattered layer of sawdust that had been there long enough to lose any of the freshness it might once have had. The front half of the room was empty of everything but a single chair and a table that held the lantern that was the guardhouse's only light. The back half was a line of half a dozen cells, each with its own cot and chamber pot tucked beneath a writing table. There was just enough room in each of them to pace three steps and turn, and that was what the prisoner was doing when Anson came in. One, two, three steps to the back wall, and around.

And when he turned to the lantern light, Anson realized why the boy's father looked shamed. He had become an informer, and the prisoner he had given up was the hedge master.

# CHAPTER

# 11

"Faith, Anson Staplyton, I'd hardly thought to be seeing you again in such a place."

"Nor I you."

"That I know. Sure, that above all things I know."

For the moment Anson forgot that he was a Fencible come to guard a prisoner, and standing his musket by the door, he went to the cell and took its bars in his hands. "It wasn't I who gave Roddy's name."

"That I know too," nodded the hedge master. "And what's more, Sorcha knows as well. She'll not be believing anything ill of you, Anson Staplyton, not for all this green world."

Anson was startled at the way those words jolted his chest.

"And she's most sorry for your trouble with your father."

"She has her own trouble. Lord Melville has evicted the O'Learys."

The hedge master nodded again.

"Do you know where she's gone?"

"I do. But perhaps just now it would be the better for you if you did not."

"Because Roddy is with her."

The hedge master said nothing.

Anson paced back and forth, as if he too were in a cell. "And what's to happen to you?" he asked suddenly.

"I'll be transported. The Dear knows it's not such a hardship. If a teacher cannot find a student wherever he goes, then he ought never to have been a teacher. It's the leaving of Ireland that's the hardship. Sure, it's the leaving of this land. But at least, Anson Staplyton, I know this: There will be hedge masters to take the place of me. There's to be no doubting of that."

The hedge master sat down on the cot and set his hands on his knees. "Do you know the story of Christy O'Duigenan over beyond Coomhola?"

Anson shook his head.

"Christy O'Duigenan went walking past Coomhola and found himself in a place he'd never seen the likes of before. The light was getting long and low when he passed a house as big as a barn and bigger, all made out of stone no moss would grow on, and past it a small village, no more than a dozen houses. 'Is there a place for a body to spend the night?' he asked in the town. 'No place but the big house,' they answered, 'and there's not been a body that's spent a night there and come out alive for as long as memory might hold.'

"'Give me six clay pipes,' he said, 'and memory will be different.' So they gave Christy O'Duigenan six clay pipes, and he went up to the house, felt his way into the sitting room through the dark, and sat down to redden one of his pipes. No sooner had he done it than a stranger sat down beside him, himself smelling of smoke. Not a single word comes out of him, then, but with a hand he strikes the pipe from Christy O'Duigenan's mouth, and it smashes against the floor. Christy O'Duigenan, he takes another pipe out, sets it between his teeth, and smokes it. The stranger smashes it again. So Christy O'Duigenan, he takes out the third pipe, and the fourth, and the fifth, and each time the stranger knocks it to pieces on the floor.

"Finally, Christy O'Duigenan takes out the sixth pipe, reddens it, and sets to smoking. And the stranger, he raises his hand to the smashing of it, but then sees that Christy O'Duigenan is never to leave in this life. So he stands and goes to the door. 'You've done me in, Christy O'Duigenan,' he says. 'The house is yours for your own self.' And Christy O'Duigenan lived there the rest of his days."

The hedge master leaned forward. "Anson Staplyton, I'm one of the clay pipes that got smashed," he said quietly. "But there will always be the next one to redden."

The next three days brought four more searches in County Dublin, all for Roderick Leary. No one came out of the houses anymore at the sound of Anson's drum. Instead, the streets filled with a sullen gray silence so loud that it muffled Anson's playing, the sound of the Fencibles' marching, and even the roared commands of Captain Brockle, who insisted that he would not be played the fool. He would have Roderick Leary in hand by month's end, he swore, and he would turn all of Dublin upside down if he must.

Between those marches, Captain Brockle held a swift and efficient military court that judged the hedge master to be a threat to His Majesty's policies in Ireland. Anson heard later from Sergeant Eyre of the unmoving acquiescence of the hedge master to the sentence that he must have expected from the moment of capture: transportation. He had made no sign whatsoever, and just once asked to speak—a request that Captain Brockle denied. He was returned to his cell until the first convict ship bound for Australia might put in to Dublin Bay. From that far country of the world, Captain Brockle had pointed out, no one ever returned.

During those three days, when not on patrol, Anson kept his own watch in the infirmary of New Barracks. He was more and more hopeful. "The colonel has his head to the wind now," assured Dr. Hoccleve. Anson had no idea what that meant, but he could see the blood-strength back in his father's face and hands, and hear the air march in and out of his father's chest as regularly and almost as smoothly as a drill on the quadrangle. Twice while he was out on patrol, his father had awakened and sipped at some soup, though he had not spoken. But when Anson sat by his cot, his eyes stayed closed.

"The sleep will swab his lungs out," Dr. Hoccleve assured him. "And see here? The color of his spittle shows no infection. He's most around the Horn now, and beating to with vengeance."

Anson assumed that this was all good news.

On the last of those three days, Anson was assigned to watch the hedge master. When he entered the guardhouse carrying a musket, he could not lift his eyes to the cell.

"Boyo," said the hedge master gently, "there's no shame in it for you."

Anson nodded.

"It is the king sitting in London town who sets the laws."

"Though," replied Anson, "it is the king's Fencibles sitting in Dublin who perform them."

"So there it is," said the hedge master. "There it is, though you may not know it yourself. The shame in your face is not just for the Fencibles, is it?"

Silence from Anson.

"You wonder," continued the hedge master, "what it is your father might have done had he been in Captain Brockle's place. And even more, you wonder what you would do if you were there."

Suddenly Anson felt himself about to weep, the tears coming out from a place deeper in him than he had ever imagined. The tears were for all those in Dublin who stood helplessly while their houses were cracked open like walnuts. And for his dreams of battlefield glory that had tarnished into a sooty and sad casting. For his father. For Sorcha's father. And even for the six men from Dundrum lying dead and buried near the low bogs of Phoenix Park.

And for the hedge master, who would never see Ireland again.

"Anson," said the hedge master gently, "the Dear knows whether you are the kind of man who would weep a family into the shame of informing, or who would transport a man for speaking his own tongue. If that is what being a Fencible is about . . ."

"No," said Anson, "that is not what a Fencible is about." He knew without a single qualm that his father would have answered the same. "But . . ." He hesitated. He suddenly felt that what he said now would stay with him forever. "My whole life I've thought of nothing but being a Fencible. If I cannot be one, then what am I to be?"

"You are to be Anson Staplyton," answered the hedge master simply. "Plant your own hedgerow. Plant it and pray God it leads as straight and true as ever it might in this tired old world."

The idea struck at Anson like nameless fear. Where once there had been order and certainty, now there was something approaching havoc. He realized that more than anything else, it was the same havoc that had been assailing him over the past three days, assailing him like an enemy more deadly than six strangers in a park. How in the name of all that is holy could he not be a Fencible? And how in the name of all that is holy could he be a Fencible?

"I too must plant my own row," said the hedge master very quietly. "And I am Ireland, as much Ireland as any man in County Dublin, loyal to King George or not. And my way is not the way of Roddy O'Leary, and neither is it the way of Colonel Staplyton. But my way in Ireland is over now, Anson Staplyton. Yours is not. By the Blessed Virgin herself, yours is not."

"I am a drummer in the Staffordshire Fencibles. I have no other way."

"Sure"—the hedge master laughed—"and what is a teacher for but to show how it is you're to be finding it?"

"And how is it that I'm to find it?"

The hedge master paused, took a deep breath, then made up his mind to his next words.

"Three ships, perhaps four by this time, lie moored at the North Quay. They carry wheat raised by Irish hands for English tables, wool spun by Irishwomen for English backs, and cattle raised off Irish land for English mouths. Come the night after next, Irishmen will burn them to the water. Now, Anson Staplyton, plant your hedgerow. Plant it straight, by the Dear."

It was a lonely planting later that night as Anson sat with his father, watching his eyes flutter open for a moment and feeling, for the first time, a return to the grip of his hand. It was just as lonely through the long night and into the gray morning's drills. And it was especially lonely at noon, when every other Fencible clamored around him at the mess.

It hardly mattered that the pork had cooked into unrecognition and that the peas were wrinkled marbles. Anson pushed them about his platter and swallowed out of reflex when he found some in his mouth. He was hardly in the mess at all, but instead out on the hills with Corporal Oakes, or in a heathered meadow with Sorcha, or on the coastline with his father, or perhaps with a bard, waiting for the sea horses to show their foaming manes in the charging waves.

Suddenly there was a laughing holler, and Anson looked up to see Sergeant Eyre at the far end of the table, swinging his arms, about to reenact a battle. The Fencibles sat, ready to listen to a tale of Fencible glory and glad somehow to be a part of it. And there was glory here, Anson knew—the glory of men who had given themselves to something larger than themselves. If it did not seem as if service in Ireland were large enough at times, there was still the memory of the regiment that could recall other days, other battles, other moments when they had stood to be the hands of empire. They had planted their hedgerows.

Out of the mess and across the quadrangle, Anson looked around at the familiar and purposeful bustle of the place, where each Fencible knew what he was about, knew what his duties were and how he should fulfill them. The patrols forming, the mounted Fencibles checking the girths and stirrups, even the Fencible lounging outside the barracks and oiling his musket—everyone on the quadrangle stitched the pattern of the Fencible's life. And Anson yearned to be a part of the stitching.

Then as he watched, a man slid out of the colonel's quarters into the bright light of the quadrangle. Anson knew him instantly: the father of the boy with the chalk. He still moved with his face lowered—even further lowered than he had several days ago. He wrapped his arms around his sides as though his ribs were about to unknit. Though he moved slowly through New Barracks, when he reached the gate he paused, looked from side to side, and then dashed off, his arms still around his sides.

The air about Anson was suddenly colder, so cold that he shivered. He would not have been amazed if snowflakes had started to careen out of the sky. If ever he had seen one, there was a man who had lost his way. Or at least been pushed out of it.

And in that moment, Anson knew what he would do with what the hedge master had told him. He would not betray those in Dundrum who had already seen their homes destroyed; he would not give them up to the brig and transportation. But neither would he betray the Fencibles and allow the ships to be burned under their watch.

He hoped that St. Gobnet would stand by him on the morrow's night, that it would be as dark as dark and any man along the North Quay as blind as if the saint had dispatched her bees.

And she did stand by him that next day, as a dark and gloomy afternoon drained itself away into a dark and gloomy night. Anson, having left his blankets stuffed with a pillow that resembled, a bit, a hunched-up and sleeping body, moved quietly down the quay. A dank fog brooded above the river, spilling over its sides and roiling over the piers. It crept up the stone docks, mounted the walls of the warehouses, and slithered onto the decks of the four ships at anchor, ready to leave with the morning's tide. If he had been a papist, Anson thought, he would have lit a rack of candles for the saint.

Hurrying along the Liffey, he shivered with the fog, and with more than the fog, watching, peering out for the light of a torch, feeling that he was absolutely alone in Dublin but knowing there were others thanking the saint for this dark night. Others who would just as soon take the ship's dirk that he carried at his side—borrowed from Dr. Hoccleve—slit him with it, and sink him into the water with four burning ships.

As he grew closer to the bay, the fog thinned some, but it confused the sounds of the night, so that sometimes his own footsteps seemed to come back to him from well ahead, and sometimes from well behind. He listened for the close marching of the patrols that Captain Brockle had sent out late in the afternoon. He should have passed one or two of them by now, since the north side of the river past Capel Street was regularly guarded. And beyond that, Captain Brockle had called out an unusual number of patrols just at dusk. Anson had seen none of them return.

He felt as if two great forces were moving out there in the fog, moving with purposeful steps toward something that they knew and could see. And his way? He was blundering between them, following a concocted plan to keep them apart. He shivered again.

Then like a fist, the prow of the first ship punched through the fog. Anson stood still and listened for the pacing of the watch, but there was none. He breathed slowly and listened again. Nothing. Had St. Gobnet been so good to him after all? A few more steps and he could see the great tarred rope that lagged across the water from the ship's bow and then wound itself about in a perfect set of coils to a tight hitch. The rope was as thick as his arm, and Anson thought that if he had to slice through it, he would have a hard night of it.

He looked over his shoulder once more, still listening. But the only sounds he heard were the stretching of the ropes and the creaking of the masts against the ships' decks.

He bent to the hitch and tugged at this loop, pushed at that, until it worked free and Anson saw the coils loosen like a live snake. He unwound the rope and let it slide noiselessly into the Liffey just as Trinity Chapel tolled one o'clock across the river.

Before the chapel had tolled the quarter hour, Anson had untied all the ropes, fore and aft, of the first three ships. He was gladdened but puzzled that it had gone so very easily, though the sweat that ran down his sides and the tightness that ached in his stomach suggested that it had not been as easy as he imagined. He could see that the first ship had already started to drift away from the quay, and that the second had her stern out into the river and would soon come around. The hitch knots on the ropes holding the last ship, however, were much tighter. Perhaps the waves out in Dublin Bay had just enough strength left in them to reach this far into the Liffey and jostle the first ship they met.

He would have to cut through the ropes.

Anson kneeled down and, with one hand wrapped about a post, leaned out over the water and began to saw at the bow line. It was soon clear that this would be a long business. By the time the half hour had struck from Trinity Chapel, he was not more than halfway through, and perhaps not even that much.

At the very moment of the last toll, a new yellow light suddenly shone against the rope. Anson turned to see where it came from and then returned feverishly to his cutting, ripping back and forth across the rope as if the banshees themselves were behind him.

But it wasn't the banshees; it was two columns of torches that came from the east and west ends of the quay, advancing with a roaring grumble and an occasional shout like the eruption of a battle. Then suddenly the shouts grew wild, and when Anson looked, he saw that the west column had confused into a rushing mob. They must have seen that the first ship was already midstream and starting to follow the tide out to the bay. The second ship too was beyond reach, at least ten or fifteen paces separating it from the dock. But the third still drifted by her moorings, and Anson knew that even the fog would not hide him from the torch-light when the crowd came upon her. That is, if the column from the east did not reach him first.

One last furious cutting, and then the river gave a tug at the ship and the rope parted. Closest to the tidal drain, the ship's fore immediately began to swing out, but it was held fast by its aft rope. There was no time to cut it. Anson dropped the dirk into the river—he would have hell to pay with Dr. Hoccleve for that—unwound two coils of rope still tied to the pier, and holding fast, jumped over the seawall and hung dangling, his eyes just on a level with the quay.

The two halves of the crowd flowed into each other and became one, thrusting their torches up and down into the air, shrilling their cries out to the ships. A few flung their torches spinning across the water at the first ship, but it was by now too far away, and the torches sizzled into the Liffey. Then the men paused, as if waiting for some sign to begin, as though reluctant to destroy what Ireland had made, even if it was on its way to England.

But the sign that came was not what they expected. Almost simultaneously, there was the shouting of orders from each of the four ships and the rumbling of rushing boots and the sharp, bright sounds of muskets struck against metal clasps as Fencibles pounded above decks. The crowd on the quay at first stilled and then roared defiance as the Fencibles took up two lines and leveled their muskets across the water. Straining at his rope and held by the shadow of the seawall, Anson now knew why the patrols had not returned. He stopped his breath as if he could hold the moment still, as if he could halt the climax of the two stalkers.

"Disperse," called Captain Brockle from the deck of the first ship. "By order of the king, disperse."

His answer was a torch lobbed across the water. As it struck the deck, a Fencible sent a musket ball tearing into the crowd, and before the officers had given the word, the Fencibles fired a volley across the water. Against them came a cascade of torches, spinning like fireworks into the night. And soon the fog was mixing together the stink of powder and singed tar, and the *pock, pock*s of the bullets sounded between the cries, the wailing cries of those hit.

The officers encouraged the firing now, and Anson felt the welter of bullets pass over his head and saw them jerk men around like invisible hammers. More torches arched toward the ships, but the crowd must have seen that the Fencibles had bucket brigades waiting for them, and no matter how many fell onto the decks, their fire did not spread.

"The rigging," someone shouted. "Torch the rigging." A barrage of cartridges rewarded his call, but he had inspired the crowd. Two, then five, then a dozen men ran forward to the edge of the quay and threw their torches high above them, each one paying for the throw with a blossoming of blood from his chest. The throws were desperate and most fell well over the ships into the river beyond. But two caught hold of the tarred ropes that lofted up to the masts, and soon the upper works of the second and fourth ships blazed up so that no one could see the stars for the sparks.

The Fencibles in the second ship began to jump overboard. Across the water came the desperate voice of Captain Brockle, but the roar of the flames and the crowd and the muskets was so loud that Anson could not make out what he was saying.

The fourth ship had swung out and away from Anson, its stern pointing to the bay. As it grew darker and darker on the quay, the light from the ship grew brighter and brighter, the fire dripping down with the melting tar, transforming the masts into flaming pillars and spreading like lava on the deck itself. The Fencibles poured a perfect frenzy of shot into the crowd to drive them back, but they would not be driven back. Again and again they surged up to the edge of the quay, and again and again the volleys would strike into them and the crowd would recoil, pulling their wounded with them.

In the silence of one of those recoils, Anson heard Trinity Chapel strike the three-quarter hour. Somewhere in this world, Anson thought, people are asleep in their beds as if the apocalypse were not upon them. And then a high-pitched, fierce cry tore at the air, and when Anson looked up, time stilled and the world held its breath.

Just above him, his right arm held back ready to throw his torch, stood Roddy O'Leary. Anson could have reached out and grabbed at his ankle. The boy stood with one leg held out stiffly, as if he had been winged. The curls of his hair had plastered themselves to his forehead, and his mouth was open to gasp at the powdered air. His hands were huge, out of proportion to the rest of him, and Anson thought, crazily enough, what a bowler he might be.

Then the world let out its breath. As Roddy's arm started to swing around, it was met with a bullet that took off the fingers of his hand and dropped the torch just past

Anson into the river. Roddy turned to look with astonishment at the ruin and swung his left hand over to hold the blood back. But it would not stay back and sprang out as though through a sieve, and when Roddy looked wildly around, he saw Anson. Desperately he held his hand out to him, but then a volley from the ship drilled a red constellation through his chest. His eyes widened with the impossibility of it, his mouth opened to cry out against death. Then, still looking at Anson, he sank like a wireless puppet and flopped onto the stones.

Another volley drove the crowd back, and then another volley directly afterward sent the crowd scurrying away. The Fencibles began to jump from the fourth ship to the quay and establish a line, and the mob rushed back into dark streets.

But Anson saw none of this. He clambered up the rope and knelt by the still form of Roddy O'Leary. He gentled the head on the stones, smoothing his curls as he did so. He tucked the ruined hand in under his jacket so he might not be shamed by it and, with his fingers, closed the eyes that flickered with the light of two burning ships.

Then he ran. He ran with the smell of Ireland's blood in his nose, the grime of gunpowder in his eyes, and the light of burning ships in his soul. Like a reckless lunatic he battered through what was left of the crowd, heedless of cries or even of pursuit, not even feeling the bullet that blazed across his shoulder. He followed the curve of the river, his breath rasping against his sprints, and whirled into the square by the Grattan Bridge.

And saw that the night's horror was not at an end.

Hanging from a makeshift gallows, a body twirled at the end of a rope. Its hands were tied behind, and its clothing torn. When the body spun slowly toward him, Anson gagged. It was the father of the boy with the chalk, and even now his face was turned to the ground in shame.

Anson ran. Crying, sputtering, he raced through the empty, fearful streets of Dublin, running as fast as if he had been mounted upon a sea horse and charging the waves, but feeling with each step the desperate energy collapsing within him.

He burst into New Barracks, retching. Haltingly, he hobbled across the stones, past the colonel's quarters, past the infirmary—he could not let his father see him so—across the open quadrangle to the barracks.

Then he stopped. Beyond the barracks squatted the low square guardhouse. Anson straightened. He looked around. The night was still dark. He gagged once more, then wiped his face twice across his sleeve. Holding himself as calmly as ever he could, he walked across and opened the door. "I'm sent to relieve you," he said to the sentry.

The sentry looked him up and down. "Trouble at the quay?"

"Trouble isn't in it," Anson answered. "You're to stand ready in case Captain Brockle sends for an additional squad."

The guard yawned and nodded. "Messy business, this." He yawned again and turned to the door. "Oh, you'll be needing these."

He handed the keys of the cells to Anson.

# 12

*C*aptain Brockle was beginning to learn the heavy weight of trying to please a patron who would not be pleased. He read once again the letter from Lord Melville that had come that morning by packet.

> *That you have taken a firm hand with miscreants suggests that I have not completely misplaced—not completely, that is—my trust in you, Captain Brockle. But a firm hand, sir, must also be a competent hand.*
>
> *I point out to you, Captain Brockle, that two of the four ships—both of which I had a very large interest in myself—were burned to the waterline, and all stores lost to recovery, if not recompense.*
>
> *I point out to you, Captain Brockle, that as the battle raged on the quay, you were caught in the ridiculous position of drifting helplessly away from your comand.*

*I point out to you, Captain Brockle, that you have found none of the rebels who might have organized such an attack.*

*I point out to you, Captain Brockle, that you have failed to protect your informant, though I do grant that it is nigh to a sin to keep faith with a papist.*

*And I most seriously point out to you, Captain Brockle, that though you have dealt with the issue of Roderick Leary, you have allowed Owen Roe Sullivan to stroll unmolested out of New Barracks to perform whatever mischief the man might wish to undertake.*

*Should you wish to enjoy my continued patronage, Captain, you will in future strive to demonstrate firmness with competence. The consequence for you otherwise might best be described as a career no better than lackluster, perhaps on the American station.*

On the American station. He might as well be off the world, for all the preferment he would find there. Captain Brockle balled the letter up in slightly trembling hands and threw it into the grate.

Damn the lord's arrogance. It was hardly his fault that the ship had drifted away. He was sure, though he could not prove, that it had been the doing of the drummer. He had seen someone clambering up the seawall; he was sure it was young Staplyton. If the ships had remained moored to the quay, his Fencibles could have surged forth and caught the lot of them. But the drummer had prevented him, though he had not prevented the fourteen corpses left behind that night.

But there was still this matter of the hedge master's escape. He had questioned the sentry and knew that the drummer had relieved him. He had let the matter simmer for two days while his Fencibles had scoured County Dublin for Sullivan. But there had been no sign.

Pacing back and forth, he decided that he would not be played for a fool and sent for Lieutenant Fielding. When he entered, the captain stood stiff and unmoving.

"Lieutenant, you were in command of New Barracks on the night of the attack?"

"I was not, sir. You will recall that you ordered patrols sent to the west of Dublin to search—"

Captain Brockle waved his hand impatiently. "Yes, yes. But had you not returned by midnight?"

"I had not, sir. Not until early the next morning."

"Do you realize, Lieutenant, how negligent it was of you to take so long? New Barracks was left without a commander."

Lieutenant Fielding said nothing.

"Do you know of the movements of the drummer during the night in question?"

"I do not, sir."

"Do you know how Sullivan escaped?"

"I do not, sir."

"By God, Lieutenant, you care little about the fulfillment of your duties. Find the drummer on the instant and send him to me. Dismissed."

Red-faced, Lieutenant Fielding saluted, turned, and left. Captain Brockle went to the window and followed him as he crossed the quadrangle on his way to the barracks. Not a Fencible he passed who did not stop with a grin and salute smartly, as if glad for a chance to be near him. He moved like a lord himself, thought Captain Brockle bitterly, and knew with more than a pang how very different it was when he walked across the quadrangle.

He watched them return together, the lieutenant with his arm on the drummer's shoulder, whispering earnestly to him. The drummer's face was grave and solemn. He was uniformed to careful precision, except his leggings were not as clean as they might be. No matter. It was not leggings he was concerned with this day. He went behind Colonel Staplyton's desk and sat down.

A knock and the drummer entered, the lieutenant behind him. Together they stood to attention, waiting for the captain to look up from the morning's dispatches. They waited while the captain pruned a quill and drafted a reply. They waited while he sealed it, stamped the seal, and then called to his aide to include it in the next set of dispatches for London.

"When will the dispatches be sent?"

"The day after tomorrow, by the turn of the morning tide, sir."

"No sooner than that?"

"No, sir."

The captain considered. "I suppose we shall have to do with that, then. Dismissed."

"Yes, sir." The aide left silently.

The captain returned to pruning his quill, and, finally satisfied with it, he laid it on his desk.

"Sir," said Lieutenant Fielding in a controlled, slow voice, "you asked to see the drummer."

Captain Brockle ignored him and instead looked directly at Anson. "You were on duty the night Owen Roe Sullivan escaped?"

"I was, sir."

"Were you the assigned sentry in the guardhouse for that night?"

"I was not, sir."

"Who assigned you to that duty, then?"

"I took it upon myself, sir."

"You took it upon yourself? Drummer, is it your opinion that the Fencibles are the sort of institution where you are encouraged to the chaos of democracy?"

"No, sir."

"You will remember, Captain," said Lieutenant Fielding, "that at the time there was no commander in New

Barracks. You yourself were drifting down the River Liffey out to Dublin Bay. A Fencible on his own must be able to make independent decisions based upon the needs of the moment."

Again Captain Brockle ignored him. "While you were in the guardhouse, the prisoner escaped."

"He did, sir."

"You will please explain how that happened, Drummer."

"I released him, sir."

A long silence followed. Captain Brockle stood, astonished. There had been no evasion, no denial. There was only the simple admission.

"You released the prisoner?"

"I did, sir."

"This too was a decision that you took upon yourself?"

"It was, sir."

"And do you realize the consequences of such a decision?"

"I do, sir. I have already drafted my resignation from the Fencibles and delivered the letter to Lieutenant Fielding."

"By God, there will be more than resignation for this. There will be an empty berth on the next transport ship now. And the offense is not above a lashing."

Lieutenant Fielding stepped forward and leaned over the desk. "Sir, the boy has already offered his resignation. With it he gives up the dream of his life. There will be no good in sending him to a colony in Australia, and there will most certainly be no good in lashing him."

"A firm hand demands otherwise."

"A clenched hand more like, and it is a clenched hand the regiment will despise."

"You speak too freely, Lieutenant."

"Captain, I speak as a Staffordshire Fencible."

Anson was hardly listening. He pushed his shoulder blades back at the thought of what the lash would do to him. He feared the flashing pain of the leather and the tearing of his skin. He feared the way the straps would wrap around his chest, and the spattering of his own blood on the cobblestones. But even more than that, he feared the ignominy of it. That a Staplyton should be lashed in front of his fellow Fencibles—it was more than could be borne.

Then he remembered that night in the brig, how he had taken the key and, as the hedge master watched silently, turned it in the lock, knowing that its turning was to change his life. He had slid the door open and then beckoned.

"And is this the row you have planted, then?" the hedge master asked.

"As best I know how."

"And does this row of yours have a name?"

Anson shook his head. "You should hurry. The squads will begin to return."

But the hedge master had not hurried. "I give your row

its name, Anson Staplyton. It is Charity." He had stood and placed his hand on Anson's head. "The Lord God carry you every road safe," he whispered. And then he was gone.

Standing now in the heat of Captain Brockle's voice, Anson reached up with his hand to the top of his head. He could almost feel the blessing, and with that, he knew some things could indeed be borne.

"You are at attention, Drummer," cried Captain Brockle. Anson snapped his hand down.

"Sir," continued Lieutenant Fielding, "I remind you respectfully that impolitic cruelty never reaps rewards."

"Drummer," said Captain Brockle, "you are relieved of all duties. From this moment forward. And you, Lieutenant, would be wise to— Yes, what is it now?"

"Sir," said Captain Brockle's aide, "Dr. Hoccleve sends word that the colonel is conscious, and not only conscious but well awake. He begs the courtesy of your presence as soon as might be convenient, and asks that the drummer accompany you."

"In due time. Tell him I will appear, but that the drummer will be unable to attend." The captain turned back to Anson. "The drummer will be confined."

And then, as if they were playing out parts of a stage play, another Fencible knocked breathlessly, and he too bore a message from the colonel.

"I am to say, sir, that as the colonel has been informed of

the events at the North Quay, you are to report to him immediately with the purpose of explaining your actions. The colonel asked me quite specifically to relate that he would brook no delay."

"Who informed the colonel of those events?"

"Sergeant Eyre has been attending the colonel this morning, sir."

Captain Brockle turned to his aide. "My coat. No, damn you, the dress coat. You, Drummer, shall attend me."

"Yes, sir."

"And you will be silent unless specifically addressed."

"Yes, sir.

"Will you stand there gawking all the day long, Lieutenant, or do you intend to pursue your duties?"

"Joy of the colonel's recovery, Anson," said Lieutenant Fielding, "and give him the regards of one who looks forward to the time when he might stand by his side in battle."

"Yes, sir. I will, sir."

The aide held out the coat. Captain Brockle roughed his arms into it, then dismissed him with a wave of his hand.

Anson stood, desperately trying to hold back the grin that threatened to break across his face. His father was conscious. A bloat of fear that had filled him these last days eased, and Anson felt instead the prickling of hot joy. He could hardly stand at attention. He could hardly not leap over the desk.

Captain Brockle adjusted the belts across his chest, studying himself in a wall mirror. Suddenly Anson felt something close to pity. In all his time in Ireland, here was the man who had risen most in the Fencibles. But it could not be seen in the curve of his back or the hunching of his shoulders. He brooded like a lonely hermit, a hermit who had retired from the world not out of devotion but out of petty fear. "Sir," said Anson, "the colonel will understand that all you have done while in command was done in service to the king."

Captain Brockle looked at him, surprised. Then his face hardened, and he turned back to the mirror with a bitter laugh. "If the colonel understands that, then tomorrow cats will fly and the moon tumble down into the sea. You know little of the ways of this world. I have saved two ships, yet two more were burned. And you have lost me my prisoner. But because of that last, boy, I am not played out yet. By God, not yet. Fall in behind me."

By now, all the Fencibles on the quadrangle had heard that the colonel was awake and demanding to see the captain. But Captain Brockle would not be seen rushing to a summons. He walked slowly, his arms clasped behind him. Anson willed him forward, a little fearful but still eager to see his father, the father with whom he had stood back to back in Phoenix Park.

Now that back was propped up by three pillows. As

soon as Anson entered the infirmary, he could hear his father's breathing—still a little raspy, but steady and without labor. His face was drawn and whiter than it should have been, and his hands lay at his sides quite still. His eyes were closed.

Captain Brockle moved to the foot of the bed and dismissed Dr. Hoccleve. Anson stood beside the colonel—he could not sit in the captain's presence—and saw that his father had been shaved and that he had donned his wig. Some of the powder from it had sprinkled the floor. "Sir," he whispered.

"Drummer," called Captain Brockle sharply, "will you learn your place?"

"My apologies, sir."

When Anson looked back at the colonel, he had opened his eyes. The drawn lines of his face vanished in a smile that broadened and broadened into something almost like glee. The colonel's hands came alive, and he pushed himself up higher against the wall. More powder sprinkled the floor, and Anson delighted in the familiar dry smell of it.

"We wheeled and faced them, did we not, boy?" The voice was thin but even.

"We did, sir."

"By God, we did. Three-to-one odds, and we lived to the telling of it."

"We'll never be able to tell Mother of it, sir."

"True enough. Nor your sisters. But what a story it will be for a grandson. By God, Anson, it will stay with me till my old age—and beyond, if heaven is the place for stodgy soldiers."

"Sir," interrupted Captain Brockle, "I am, as you must be aware, temporarily in command of the regiment, and so have more than a few duties to attend."

The colonel's face leaned and reddened. "Any more important, Captain, than a summons from your colonel?"

"No, sir."

"You are now most certainly aware that under the present circumstances, you are to take no action on behalf of the regiment without consulting me."

"I am aware of that, sir."

The colonel shifted his back against the pillows. "Then, Captain, to the matter of the North Quay."

"It was a matter perfect in its conception but befouled in its execution. Had the ships not been loosed from the quay"—Captain Brockle glared at Anson as he said this—"we would have been able to bring more guns to bear. As it was, only two of the ships were lost, sir. Two were preserved."

"Captain, I hardly give a fig for Lord Melville's ships. Tell me, what is the cost in lives of your expedition?"

"Not a single Fencible so much as wounded, sir."

"In lives, Captain."

"Fourteen rebels killed, sir."

"Do you count the man hanged on Capel Street?"

"That, sir, was none of our doing."

"It was of our doing, Captain. He was a man to whom I had given my word of honor. And you, Captain, speaking in my place, took it upon yourself to revoke that word and destroy him. No, Captain, do not evade what the Fencibles have done to this man. We have destroyed him."

"Sir, as you are already informed of these particulars, perhaps there is no further need for my attendance."

"Stand at attention, Captain. Captain, as a military man, tell me: Is Dublin more or less loyal to the king since you took command of the Fencibles?"

"Sir, we were instructed to act with a firm hand. This is what I have done."

"And your firm hand has taken us to a place where one man looks into another's face and is fearful to speak, lest he be speaking to a scum of an informant. To a place where Fencibles shoot not to defend the king's subjects but to defend a cargo of wheat and wool."

"May I remind you, sir, that you yourself were attacked?"

"By God, sir, you are impertinent. And I shall break you for it. For overreaching your command. For utter incompetence in the field. For subverting the peace."

"Sir," said the captain, "there is another matter."

"And what is that, Captain?"

"There is the loss of the prisoner, Owen Roe Sullivan."

"Tell me about that loss, Captain."

Captain Brockle held his hand out toward Anson. "Perhaps, sir, your son might speak to this matter, as he is better informed on it than I."

The colonel turned to Anson and waited. Anson took a deep breath. "Sir, I released the prisoner."

"Indeed. And for what cause?"

"Because, sir, Ireland will never be part of the empire if it must first cease to be itself. And no number of Fencibles can force the first—nor, for that matter, the last."

"This conclusion you have come to in defiance of all the king's counselors and ministers."

"I have, sir."

"And so you have acted upon it as a Fencible."

"I have acted upon it as my own way, sir. It is the only way I must and can act."

"That is not the language of a Fencible."

"I have already submitted my resignation to Lieutenant Fielding, sir." Anson did not drop his eyes. He was not ashamed of what he had done, but he did expect bitter disappointment from the colonel. The long line of Staplytons who had taken up the king's uniform as Fencibles would be broken, and he knew his father might despise him for it. He hardly knew if he might despise himself.

"Sir," said Captain Brockle, "this is no slight offense." His voice was edged with something like panic, and once again Anson felt the stirrings of pity for the man. His whole career—his whole life, he thought—balanced on the fulcrum of this next moment.

"It is no slight offense," agreed the colonel.

"Transportation would not be inappropriate."

"You undoubtedly move to a point, Captain."

The captain nodded. A hand wiped across his mouth, and Anson wondered if he was even aware of it. "My point, sir, is that perhaps this most unhappy affair should not occupy us longer. The events on the North Quay and those in the guardhouse that night need not have permanent consequences."

"For either of you."

"As you say, sir." The captain inclined his head in a slight bow.

The colonel was silent for a long time. Then he spoke with resignation in his voice. "Then we shall leave it at that, Captain."

Relief crossed Captain Brockle's face. But when he looked at Anson, relief gave way to a hard bitterness. He was a man who had tasted the sweetness of command. Now he had wheedled himself from being broken, and he hated those who had taken the sweetness away. Anson watched the bitterness stiffen around him like a patina.

"Perhaps, Captain Brockle, you had best retire to the duties you spoke of earlier."

"Good morning, then, sir." He said it as a malediction.

"Good morning, Captain." And Captain Brockle left the infirmary, trying not to move too quickly but hardly able to slow his hastening feet.

The colonel laid his head back against the pillows. Another sprinkle of powder on the floor. He closed his eyes, and Anson waited silently for them to open again and for the accompanying bellows to begin. A family tradition of generations gone to rot, all for a belief that Anson himself could only half articulate. And to make matters worse, it was a belief that his father, a Fencible, could not possibly accept.

Anson held back his shoulders against the heaviness of the silence and waited. Then his father's eyes opened. He turned his head to Anson. And he did the one thing that Anson could never have expected, something that astonished him. It seemed to him that he was standing in the presence of a miracle so vast that it could hardly be conceived.

The colonel was laughing.

He was laughing great belly laughs, holding his hand over his mouth to keep from guffawing, grimacing at the deeper laughs that pulled at the wounded muscles of his chest, but unable to stop.

"Pardon, boy, pardon," he said, and then broke again into a glad laughter that infected even Anson, who smiled through his confusion. "Pardon me," he said again, "but that fellow is such a predictable scoundrel."

And then Anson knew. "By God," he said wonderingly, "if you are not something of a scoundrel yourself. You knew everything before we came in here."

"I did."

"And you manipulated it so that the captain would not press matters against me."

"Caught in the very act. Though, Anson, the sergeant too must claim some part of the mischief." He began to laugh again, holding his arms tight across his chest against the pain.

Anson did not know whether to laugh or stand at attention. There would be no lashing. But neither would there be a career in the Fencibles. He felt oddly blank.

The colonel quieted and their eyes met. "So, Anson, in finding your own way, as you put it, you have committed a serious act as a Fencible."

"My resignation is sincere, sir."

"As it must be. Perhaps there are times when the honor of a Fencible demands that he must no longer be a Fencible."

"And you, sir?"

The colonel looked at him a moment, and when he spoke, his voice was halting. "You have found your way; I mine. Mine is and must be the way of the Fencibles. Yours is not. And perhaps it is for the best. You never could keep your leggings in a state anything close to acceptable." A smile crossed his face and he blinked his eyes, then blinked them again. He held out his hand to his son, and Anson took it and felt the hard grasp of a Fencible officer, the firm hold of his father. "By God, Anson," the colonel said, "we did wheel and face them."

For Anson, all the rest of the world pulled back, leaving just the two of them alone in its spacious center, and that was enough. He held his father's hand as if it were a newly discovered treasure, all the more precious for having been sought for a very long time.

Two mornings later Anson stood by the rail of the *Fortune*, absent his red coat, fastening firmly to his memory the sight of his father, Lieutenant Fielding, and Sergeant Eyre standing on the quay. Behind them a squad of Fencibles stood guard, a sign of the task his father faced if there was ever to be peace in Ireland. If it was a task that a Fencible might master, then his father would do it.

The tide gripped the *Fortune* and brought her out into the Liffey, but for Anson it was as if he were standing still and the quay receding from him. His life as a Fencible was over, and he stood as one between two dreams, the first one lost, the second unknown. He saw the lieutenant and sergeant back away from the colonel to leave him alone in this final moment, and in that moment Anson stood to attention and saluted. The colonel saluted in return, and so the river parted them to their own ways.

But Anson could not let go yet. As the business of

preparing for a sea crossing scurried the sailors about the deck, Anson retreated to the stern, where he watched the streets of Dublin pass by, one by one. The Liffey began to broaden out farther and farther, until he could no longer be sure whether he was in the river or in the bay, except that the horizon had started to pull the edges of the land back to itself.

And then, on the nearest headland that the south hills dropped down, he saw them. The hedge master, his arms high in the air, waving and waving at the *Fortune*. And beside him stood—it must be—Sorcha. And she too was waving. Waving for all she was worth. Anson threw his own arms into the air and waved wildly back and forth, waving with all the painful gladness that filled his soul. "The Lord God carry you every road safe," he called to them. "The Lord God carry you."

So they stood, their arms high, as the wind big-bellied the sails, the wake of the *Fortune* turned white, and the land hazed to a blue in Anson's clear eye.

# About the Author

GARY D. SCHMIDT and his wife live on a one-hundred-fifty-year-old farm in Alto, Michigan, where, together with their six children, they raise vegetables for food, hardwoods for heat, venerable oaks for history, and two—or three—dogs for pleasure. When Gary is not doing the raising, he is either teaching at Calvin College or writing.

His first novel, *The Sin Eater*, an ALA Best Book for Young Adults, explored his interest in how family stories tell us about our forgotten past. It was a similar interest that led him to Irish hedge masters, for they too fought to hold onto a culture and a life that was forced to disappear.

In addition to studies of writers of children's literature such as Katherine Paterson, Hugh Lofting, Robert Lawson, and Robert McCloskey, Gary has retold Biblical tales in *The Blessing of the Lord* and a saint's tale in *St. Ciarin*, all written on his 1953 Royal typewriter. His family worries that he will never master the next millennium's technology. He worries that he will not be able to find typewriter ribbons for very much longer.